THE ATHEIST'S MASS

HONORÉ DE BALZAC

THE ATHEIST'S MASS

TRANSLATED BY SYLVIA RAPHAEL

PENGUIN BOOKS

PENGUIN BOOKS

Published by the Penguin Group
Penguin Books USA Inc., 375 Hudson Street,
New York, New York 10014, U.S.A.
Penguin Books Ltd, 27 Wrights Lane,
London W8 5TZ, England
Penguin Books Australia Ltd, Ringwood,
Victoria, Australia
Penguin Books Canada Ltd, 10 Alcorn Avenue,
Toronto, Ontario, Canada M4V 3B2
Penguin Books (N.Z.) Ltd, 182–190 Wairau Road,
Auckland 10, New Zealand

Penguin Books Ltd, Registered Offices:
Harmondsworth, Middlesex, England

Published in Penguin Books 1995

Translation copyright © Sylvia Raphael, 1977
All rights reserved

These selections are from *Selected Short Stories*,
translated by Sylvia Raphael, published by Penguin Books.

ISBN 0 14 60.0199 0

Printed in the United States of America

CONTENTS

The Atheist's Mass

A doctor to whom science owes a fine physiological theory and who, while still young, achieved a place amongst the celebrities of the Paris school of medicine (that centre of enlightenment to which all the doctors of Europe pay homage), Doctor Bianchon, practised surgery for a long time before devoting himself to medicine. His early studies were directed by one of the greatest of French surgeons, by the celebrated Desplein who passed through the world of science like a meteor. Even his enemies admit that he took with him to the grave a method that could not be handed on to others. Like all men of genius he had no heirs; he carried his skill within him and he carried it away with him. A surgeon's fame is like an actor's. It exists only so long as he is alive and his talent can no longer be appreciated once he has gone. Actors and surgeons, great singers too, and virtuoso musicians who by their playing increase tenfold the power of music, are all heroes of the moment. Desplein's life is a proof of the resemblance between the destinies of these transitory geniuses. His name which was so famous yesterday is almost forgotten today. It will remain only in his own field without going beyond it. But extraordinary conditions are surely necessary for the name of a scholar to pass from the domain of Science into the general history of humanity. Did Desplein have that width of knowledge which makes a man the mouthpiece or the representative of an age? Desplein possessed a god-like glance; he understood the patient and his disease by means of a natural or acquired intuition which allowed him to appreciate the diagnosis appropriate to the individual, to decide the precise moment, the hour, the minute at which he should operate, taking into account atmospheric conditions and temperamental peculiarities. To be able to collaborate with Nature in this way, had he then studied the endless combination of beings and elemental substances contained in the atmosphere or provided by the earth for man, who absorbs them and uses them for a particular purpose? Did he use that power of deduction and analogy to which Cuvier owes his genius? However that may be, this man understood the secrets of the flesh; he understood its past as well as its future, by studying the present. But did he contain all science in his person as did Hippocrates, Galen, Aristotle? Did he lead a whole school towards new worlds? No. If it is impossible to refuse to this constant observer of human chemistry the ancient science of Magism, that is to say, the knowledge of the elements in fusion, of the causes of life, of life before life, of what it will be, judging from its antecedents before it exists, all this unfortunately was personal to him. In his life he was isolated by egoism, and today that egoism is the death of his fame. Over his tomb there is no statue proclaiming to the future, in ringing tones, the mysteries which Genius seeks out at its own expense. But perhaps Desplein's talent was in keeping with his beliefs, and consequently mortal. For him the terrestrial atmosphere was like a generative bag; he saw the earth as if it were an egg in its shell, and unable to know whether the egg or the hen came first, he denied both the fowl and the egg. He believed neither in the animal anterior to man nor in the spirit beyond him. Desplein was not in doubt, he affirmed his opinion. He was like many other scholars in his frank, unmixed atheism. They are the best people in the world but incorrigible atheists, atheists such as religious people don't believe exist. It was hardly possible for such a man to hold a different opinion, for from his youth he was used to dissecting the living being *par excellence*, before, during and after life, and to examining all its functions without finding the unique soul that is indispensable to religious theories. Desplein recognized a cerebral centre, a nervous centre and a circulatory centre, of which the first two do duty for each other so well that at the end of his life he was convinced that the sense of hearing was not absolutely necessary to hear, nor the sense of sight absolutely necessary to see, and that the solar plexus could replace them without anyone noticing it. He thus found two souls in man and this fact confirmed his atheism, although it still tells us nothing about God. He died, they say, impenitent to the last, as unfortunately do many fine geniuses. May God forgive them!

This really great man's life exhibited many pettinesses, to use the expression of his enemies who in their jealousy wanted to diminish his fame, but it would be more appropriate to call them apparent contradictions. Envious or stupid people who do not know the reasons which explain the activities of superior minds immediately take advantage of a few superficial contradictions to make accusations on which they obtain a momentary judgement. If, later on, the plans which have been attacked are crowned with success, when the preparations are correlated with the results, some of the calumnies which were made beforehand remain. Thus, in our own time, Napoleon was condemned by our contemporaries when he spread out the wings of his eagle over England: but we needed the events of 1822 to explain 1804 and the flat-bottomed boats at Boulogne.

Since Desplein's fame and scientific knowledge were unassailable, his enemies attacked his strange disposition and his character, while in fact he was simply what the English call eccentric. At times he dressed magnificently like the tragedian Crébillon, at times he seemed unusually indifferent to clothes. Sometimes he was to be seen in a carriage, sometimes on foot. He was now sharp-tempered, now kind, apparently hard and stingy, yet capable of offering his fortune to his exiled rulers who honoured him by accepting it for a few days. No man has inspired more contradictory judgements. Although, to obtain the Order of Saint Michael (which doctors are not supposed to solicit), he was capable of dropping a Book of Hours from his pocket at Court, you can be sure that inwardly he laughed at the whole thing. He had a profound contempt for mankind, having studied them from above and from below, having surprised them without pretence, as they performed the most solemn as well as the pettiest acts of life. A great man's gifts often hang together. If one of these giants has more talent than wit, his wit is still greater than that of a man of whom one says simply, 'He is witty.' All genius presupposes moral insight. This insight may be applied to some speciality, but he who sees the flower must see the sun. The doctor who heard a diplomat whose life he had saved ask, 'How is the Emperor?', and who replied, 'The courtier is coming back to life, the man will follow!' was not only a surgeon or a physician, he was also extremely witty. Thus the close and patient observer of humanity will justify

4

Desplein's exorbitant pretensions and will realize, as he himself realized, that he was capable of being as great a minister as he was a surgeon.

Among the riddles which Desplein's life reveals to his contemporaries we have chosen one of the most interesting, because the solution will be found at the end of this tale and will answer some of the foolish accusations which have been made against him.

Of all the pupils whom Desplein had at his hospital, Horace Bianchon was one of those to whom he became most warmly attached. Before doing his internship at the Hôtel Dieu, Horace Bianchon was a medical student, living in a miserable boarding-house in the Latin Quarter, known by the name of La Maison Vauquer. There this poor young man experienced that desperate poverty which is a kind of melting-pot whence great talents emerge pure and incorruptible, just as diamonds can be subjected to any kind of shock without breaking. In the violence of their unleashed passions, they acquire the most unshakeable honesty, and by dint of the constant labour with which they have contained their balked appetites, they become used to the struggles which are the lot of genius. Horace was an upright young man, incapable of double-dealing in affairs of honour, going straight to the point without fuss, as capable of pawning his coat for his friends as of giving them his time and his night's rest. In short, Horace was one of those friends who are not worried about what they receive in exchange for what they give, certain as they are to receive in their turn more than they will give. Most of his friends had for him that inner respect which is inspired by unostentatious goodness, and several of them were afraid of his strictures. But Horace exercised these virtues without being prudish. He was neither a puritan nor a preacher; he swore quite readily when giving advice, and enjoyed a good meal in gay company when opportunity offered. He was good company, no more squeamish than a soldier, bluff and open, not like a sailor — for the sailor of today is a wily diplomatist — but like a fine young man who has nothing to hide in his life; he walked with his head high and his heart light. In a word, Horace was the Pylades of more than one Orestes, creditors being today the most real shape assumed by the ancient Furies. He wore his poverty with that gaiety which is perhaps one of the greatest elements of courage, and like all those who have nothing, he contracted few debts. Sober as a camel, brisk as a stag, he was unwavering both in his principles and in his behaviour. The happiness of Bianchon's life began on the day when the famous surgeon obtained evidence of the good qualities and failings which, the one as much as the other, made Doctor Horace Bianchon doubly precious to his friends. When a clinical chief adopts a young man, that young man has, as they say, his foot in the stirrup. Desplein always took Bianchon with him to act as his assistant in well-to-do homes, where some reward would nearly always find its way into the student's purse, and where little by little the mysteries of Parisian life were revealed to the young provincial. Desplein also kept him in his surgery during consultations and gave him work to do there. Sometimes he would send him to accompany a rich patient to a spa. In short, he was making a practice for him. The result of all this was that after a time the lord of surgery had a devoted slave. These two men, the one at the height of his fame and leader of his profession, enjoying an immense fortune and an immense reputation, the other, a modest Omega, having neither fortune nor fame, became intimate friends. The great Desplein told his assistant everything. He knew if a certain lady had sat down on a chair beside the master, or on the famous surgery couch where Desplein slept. Bianchon knew the mysteries of that temperament, both lion-like and bull-like, which in the end expanded and abnormally developed the great man's chest and caused his death from enlargement of the heart. The student studied the eccentricities of Desplein's very busy life, the plans made by his sordid avarice, the hopes of the politician concealed behind the scientist; he foresaw the disappointments in store for the only feeling hidden in that heart which was hardened rather than hard.

One day Bianchon told Desplein that a poor water-carrier from the Saint-Jacques quarter had a horrible illness caused by fatigue and poverty; this poor Auvergnat had eaten only potatoes during the severe winter of 1821. Desplein left all his patients. At the risk of working his horse to death, he rode as fast as he could, followed by Bianchon, to the poor man's house and himself had him carried to the nursing-home founded by the famous Dubois in the Faubourg Saint-Denis. Desplein attended the man, and when he had cured him, gave him the money to buy a horse and a water-cart. This Auvergnat was remarkable for one original characteristic. One of his friends fell ill; he took him straight away to Desplein and said to his benefactor, 'I would not have allowed him to go to another doctor.' Surly as he was, Desplein grasped the water-carrier's hand and said, 'Bring them all to me.' And he had the peasant from the Cantal admitted to the Hôtel Dieu, where he took the greatest care of him. Bianchon had already noticed several times that his chief had a predilection for Auvergnats, and especially for water-carriers. But as Desplein had a kind of pride in his treatments at the Hôtel Dieu, his pupil didn't see anything very strange in that.

One day, as Bianchon was crossing the Place Saint-Sulpice, he noticed his master going into the church about nine o'clock in the morning. Desplein, who at that period of his life never moved a step except by carriage, was on foot and slipping in by the door of the Rue du Petit-Lion, as if he had been going into a house of doubtful reputation. Bianchon's curiosity was naturally aroused, since he knew his master's opinions and that he was a 'devyl' of a Cabanist (devyl with a y, which in Rabelais seems to suggest a superiority in devilry). Slipping into Saint-Sulpice, he was not a little astonished to see the great Desplein, that atheist without pity for the angels, who cannot be subjected to the surgeon's knife, who cannot have sinus or gastric trouble, that dauntless scoffer, kneeling humbly, and where? ... in the chapel of the Virgin, where he listened to a Mass, paid for the cost of the service, gave alms for the poor, all as solemnly as if he had been performing an operation.

'He certainly didn't come to clear up questions about the Virgin birth,' said Bianchon in boundless astonishment. 'If I had seen him holding one of the tassels of the canopy on Corpus Christi day, I would have taken it as a joke; but at this hour, alone, with no one to see him, that certainly gives one food for thought!'

Bianchon did not want to look as if he was spying on the

chief surgeon of the Hôtel Dieu and he went away. By chance Desplein invited him to dinner that very day, not at home but at a restaurant.

Between the fruit and the cheese, Bianchon managed skilfully to bring the conversation round to the subject of the Mass, calling it a masquerade and a farce.

'A farce,' said Desplein, 'which has cost Christendom more blood than all Napoleon's battles and all Broussais' leeches! The Mass is a papal invention which goes no further back than the sixth century and which is based on *Hoc est corpus*. What torrents of blood had to be spilt to establish Corpus Christi day! By the institution of this Feast the court of Rome intended to proclaim its victory in the matter of the Real Presence, a schism which troubled the Church for three centuries. The wars of the Counts of Toulouse and the Albigensians are the tail-end of this affair. The Vaudois and the Albigensians refused to recognize this innovation.'

In short Desplein enjoyed himself, giving free rein to his atheistic wit, and pouring out a flood of Voltairean jokes, or, to be more precise, a horrible parody of the *Citateur*.

'Well,' Bianchon said to himself, 'where is the pious man I saw this morning?'

He said nothing; he had doubts whether he really had seen his chief at Saint-Sulpice. Desplein would not have bothered to lie to Bianchon. They both knew each other too well; they had already exchanged ideas on subjects which were just as serious, and they had discussed systems *de natura rerum*, probing or dissecting them with the knives and the scalpel of incredulity. Three months went by. Bianchon did not follow up the incident, although it remained stamped on his memory. One day in the course of that year, one of the doctors at the Hôtel Dieu took Desplein by the arm, in Bianchon's presence, as if to ask him a question.

'What were you going to do at Saint-Sulpice, my dear chief?' he asked.

'I went to see a priest who had a diseased knee. Madame la Duchesse d'Angoulême did me the honour of recommending me,' said Desplein.

The doctor was satisfied with this excuse, but not so Bianchon.

'Oh! So he goes to see bad knees in church! He was going to hear Mass,' the student said to himself.

Bianchon determined to keep a watch on Desplein. He recalled the day and the time on which he had surprised him going in to Saint-Sulpice and he determined to go there the following year on the same day and at the same time, to find out if he would surprise him there again. If that happened, the regularity of his worship would justify a scientific investigation, for in such a man there should not be a direct contradiction between thought and deed. The following year, on the day and at the hour in question, Bianchon, who was by this time no longer Desplein's assistant, saw the surgeon's carriage stop at the corner of the Rue de Tournon and the Rue du Petit-Lion. From there his friend crept stealthily along by the walls of Saint-Sulpice where he again heard Mass at the altar of the Virgin. It was certainly Desplein, the chief surgeon, the atheist *in petto*, the pious man on occasion. The plot became more involved. The famous scientist's persistence complicated everything. When Desplein had left the church, Bianchon went up to the sacristan who came to minister to the chapel, and asked him if the gentleman was a regular attendant.

'I have been here for twenty years,' said the sacristan, 'and for all that time Monsieur Desplein has been coming four times a year to hear this Mass; it was he who founded it.'

'*He* founded it!' said Bianchon as he walked away. 'This is as much a mystery as the Immaculate Conception, which of itself must make a doctor an unbeliever.'

Although Dr Bianchon was a friend of Desplein's, some time went by before he was in a position to speak to him about this strange circumstance of his life. If they met at a consultation or in society, it was difficult to find that moment of confidence and solitude when, with feet up on the fire-dogs and heads leaning against the backs of their chairs, two men tell each other their secrets. Finally, seven years later, after the 1830 Revolution, when the people stormed the Archbishopric, when, inspired by Republican sentiments, they destroyed the golden crosses which appeared, like flashes of lightning, in this vast sea of houses, when Disbelief and Violence swaggered together through the streets, Bianchon surprised Desplein going into Saint-Sulpice. The doctor followed him in and took a place near him without his friend making the least sign or showing the least surprise. Both of them heard the foundation Mass.

'Will you tell me, my friend,' Bianchon said to Desplein when they were outside the church, 'the reason for this display of piety? I have already caught you three times going to Mass, you! You must tell me the reason for this mysterious activity, and explain to me the flagrant discrepancy between your opinions and your behaviour. You don't believe in God, yet you go to Mass! My dear chief, you must answer me.'

'I am like many pious men, men who appear to be profoundly religious but are quite as atheistic as we are, you and I.'

And he let forth a torrent of epigrams about political personalities of whom the best known provides us in this century with a new edition of Molière's *Tartuffe*.

'That's not what I am talking about,' said Bianchon. 'I want to know the reason for what you have just been doing here. Why did you found this Mass?'

'Well, my dear friend,' said Desplein, 'since I am on the brink of the grave, there is no reason why I shouldn't speak to you about the beginning of my life.'

At this moment Bianchon and the great man happened to be in the Rue des Quatre-Vents, one of the most horrible streets in Paris. Desplein pointed to the sixth storey of one of those houses which are shaped like an obelisk and have a medium-sized door opening on to a passage. At the end of the passage is a spiral staircase lit by apertures called *jours de souffrance*. The house was a greenish colour; on the ground floor lived a furniture dealer; a different kind of poverty seemed to lodge on each floor. Raising his arm with an emphatic gesture, Desplein said to Bianchon, 'I lived up there for two years.'

'I know the place; d'Arthez lived there and I came here almost every day in my youth. At that time we called it the "jar of great men"! Well, what of it?'

'The Mass that I have just heard is linked to events which took place at the time when I lived in the attic where, so you tell me, d'Arthez lived. It is the one where a line of washing is dangling at the window above a pot of flowers. I had such a difficult time to start with, my dear Bianchon, that I can dispute the palm of the sufferings of Paris with anyone. I have put up with everything, hunger, thirst, lack of money, lack of clothes, of footwear, of linen, everything that is hardest about poverty. I have blown on my numbed fingers in that "jar of great men" which I should like to visit again with you. I worked during one winter, when I could see my own head steaming and a cloud of my own breath rising like horses' breath on a frosty day. I don't know what enables a man to stand up to such a life. I was alone, without help, without a farthing either to buy books or to pay the expenses of my medical education. I had no friends and my irritable, sensitive, restless temperament did me no good. No one could see that my bad temper was caused by the difficulties and the work of a man who, from his position at the bottom of the social ladder, was striving to reach the top. But I can tell *you*, you to whom I don't need to pretend, that I had that basis of good feeling and keen sensitivity which will always be the prerogative of men who, after having been stuck for a long time in the slough of poverty, are strong enough to climb to any kind of summit. I could get nothing from my family or my home beyond the inadequate allowance they made me. In short, at this period of my life, all I had to eat in the mornings was a roll which the baker in the Rue du Petit-Lion sold me more cheaply because it was yesterday's, or the day before yesterday's. I crumbled it up into some milk and so my morning meal cost me only two sous. I dined only every other day at a boarding-house where dinner cost sixteen sous. In this way I spent only nine sous a day. You know as well as I do the care I had to take of my clothes and my footwear. I don't think, later on in life, we are as much distressed by a colleague's disloyalty as you and I were when we saw the mocking grin of a shoe that was becoming unsewn, or heard the armhole of a frock-coat split. I drank only water; I had the greatest respect for cafés. Zoppi's seemed to me like a promised land which the Luculli of the Latin Quarter alone had the right to patronize. Sometimes I wondered whether I would ever be able to have a cup of white coffee there, or play a game of dominoes. In short, I transferred to my work the fury which poverty inspired in me. I tried to master scientific knowledge so that I should have an immense personal worth deserving of the place I would reach when I emerged from my obscurity. I consumed more oil than bread; the light which lit up those stubborn vigils cost me more than my food. The struggle was long, hard and unrelieved. I aroused no feelings of friendship in those around me. To make friends, you must mix with young people, have a few sous so that you can go and have a drink with them, go with them everywhere where students go. I had nothing. And no one in Paris realizes that "nothing" is "nothing". When there was any question of revealing my poverty I experienced that nervous contraction of the throat which makes our patients think that a ball is rising up from the gullet into the larynx. Later on I met people who, born rich and never having lacked for anything, don't know the problem of this rule of three: "A young man is to crime as a hundred sous piece is to X." These gilded fools say to me, "Why did you get into debt? Why did you take on such crushing obligations?" They remind me of the princess who, knowing that the people were dying of hunger, asked, "Why don't they buy cake?" I should very much like to see one of those rich people, who complains that I charge too much for operating on him, alone in Paris, without a penny, without a friend, without credit and forced to work with his two hands to live. What would he do? Where would he satisfy his hunger? Bianchon, if at times you have seen me bitter and hard, it was because I was superimposing my early sufferings on the lack of feeling, the selfishness, of which I had thousands of examples in high places; or I was thinking of the obstacles which hatred, envy, jealousy, and calumny have placed between me and success. In Paris, when certain people see you ready to put your foot in the stirrup, some of them pull you back by the coat-tail, others loosen the buckle of the saddle-girth so that you'll fall and break your head; this one takes the shoes of your horse, that one steals your whip. The least treacherous is the one you see coming up to shoot you at point-blank range. You have enough talent, my dear fellow, soon to be acquainted with the horrible, unending battle which mediocrity wages against superiority. If one evening you lose twenty-five louis, the next day you will be accused of being a gambler and your best friends will say that the day before you lost twenty-five thousand francs. If you have a headache, you will be called a lunatic. If you have one outburst of temper, they will say you are a social misfit. If, in order to resist this army of pygmies, you muster your superior forces, your best friends will cry out that you want to eat up everything, that you claim to have the right to dominate and lord it over others. In short, your good qualities will become failings, your failings will become vices, and your virtues will be crimes. If you have saved a man, they'll say you have killed him; if your patient is in circulation again, they will affirm that you have sacrificed the future to the present; if he is not dead, he will die. Hesitate, and you will be lost! Invent anything at all, claim your just due, you will be regarded as a sly character, difficult to deal with, who is standing in the way of the young men. So, my dear fellow, if I don't believe in God, I believe still less in man. You recognize in me a Desplein very different from the Desplein everyone speaks ill of, don't you? But let's not rummage in this muck heap. Well, I used to live in this house; I was busy working to pass my first examination and I hadn't a sou. I had reached one of those extreme situations where, you know, a man says to himself, "I shall join the army." I had one last hope. I was expecting from home a trunk full of linen, a present from old aunts of the kind who, knowing nothing of Paris, think of your shirts and imagine that with thirty francs a month their nephew lives on caviar. The trunk arrived while I was at the school; the carriage cost forty francs. The porter, a German cobbler who lived in a garret, had paid the money and was keeping the trunk. I went for a walk in the Rue des Fossés-Saint-Germain-des-Prés and in the Rue de l'Ecole-de-Médecine, but I could not think up a plan which would deliver my trunk to me without my having to pay the forty francs; naturally I would have paid them after I had sold the linen. My stupidity made me realize that I was gifted for nothing but surgery. My dear fellow, sensitive souls whose gifts are deployed in a lofty sphere are lacking in that spirit of intrigue which is so resourceful in contriving schemes. *Their* genius lies in chance; they don't seek for things, they come on them by chance. Well, I returned at nightfall at the same time that my neighbour, a water-carrier named Bourgeat, a man from Saint-Flour, was going home. We knew each other in the way two tenants do who have rooms on the same landing, and who hear each other sleeping, coughing, and dressing, till in the end they get used to one another. My neighbour informed me that the landlord, to whom I owed three quarters' rent, had turned me out; I would have to clear out the next day. He himself had been given notice because of his calling. I spent the most unhappy night of my life. Where would I find a carrier to remove my poor household affairs and my books? How would I be able to pay the carrier and the porter? Where was I to go? I kept on asking myself these unanswerable questions through my tears, like a madman repeating a refrain. I fell asleep. Poverty has in its favour an exquisite sleep filled with beautiful dreams. The next morning, just as I was eating my bowlful of crumbled bread and milk, Bourgeat came in and said in his bad French, "*Monchieur l'étudiant*, I'm a poor man, a foundling from the Chain-Flour hospital. I've no father or mother and I'm not rich enough to get married. You haven't many relations either, or much in the way of hard cash. Now listen. I've got a hand-cart downstairs which I've hired for two *chous* an hour. It'll take all our things. If you're willing, we'll look for digs together since we're turned out of here. After all, this place isn't an earthly paradise."

"'I know that all right, Bourgeat, my good fellow,' I replied. "But I'm in rather a jam. Downstairs I have a trunk containing linen worth a hundred crowns. With that I could pay the landlord and what I owe the porter, but I haven't got a hundred sous."

'"That doesn't matter, I've got some cash," Bourgeat replied cheerfully, showing me a filthy old leather purse. "Keep your linen."

'Bourgeat paid my three quarters' rent and his own and settled with the porter. Then he put our furniture and my linen on to his cart and dragged it through the streets, stopping in front of every house which had a "to let" sign hanging out. My job was to go up and see if the place to let would suit us. At midday we were still wandering about the Latin Quarter without having found anything. The price was a great difficulty. Bourgeat suggested that we should have lunch at a wine-shop; we left our cart at the door. Towards evening, I discovered in the Cour de Rohan, Passage du Commerce, two rooms, separated by the stair in the attic at the top of a house. The rent was sixty francs a year each. We were housed at last, my humble friend and I. We had dinner together. Bourgeat, who earned about fifty sous a day, had about a hundred crowns. He was soon going to be able to realize his ambition and buy a water-cart and a horse. When he learned about my situation (for he dragged my secrets out of me with a deep cunning and a good nature the memory of which still touches my heart), he gave up for some time his whole life's ambition. Bourgeat had been a street-merchant for twenty-two years; he sacrificed his hundred crowns to my future.'

Desplein gripped Bianchon's arm with emotion.

'He gave me the money I needed for my exams. My friend, that man realized that I had a mission, that the needs of my intelligence were more important than his own. He took care of me; he called me his child and lent me the money I needed to buy books. Sometimes he would come in very quietly to watch me working. Last but not least, he took care, as a mother might have done, to see that instead of the bad and insufficient food which I had been forced to put up with, I had a healthy and plentiful diet. Bourgeat, who was a man of about forty, had the face of a medieval burgess, a dome-like forehead and a head that a painter might have used as a model for Lycurgus. The poor man's heart was filled with affections which had no outlet. The only creature that had ever loved him was a poodle which had died a short time before. He talked to me continually about it and asked me if I thought that the Church would be willing to say Masses for the repose of its soul. His dog was, so he said, a true Christian and it had gone to church with him for twelve years, without ever barking there. It had listened to the organ without opening its mouth and squatted beside him with a look that made him think it was praying with him. This man transferred all his affections to me; he accepted me as a lonely and unhappy creature. He became for me the most attentive of mothers, the most tactful of benefactors, in short, the ideal of that virtue which delights in its own work. Whenever I met him in the street, he would glance at me with an understanding look filled with remarkable nobility; then he would pretend to walk as if he was carrying nothing. He seemed happy to see me in good health and well-dressed. In short, it was the devotion of a man of the people, the love of a working-girl transferred to a higher sphere. Bourgeat did my errands; he woke me up at night at the hours I asked him to. He cleaned my lamp and polished our landing. He was as good a servant as he was a father, and tidy as an English girl. He did the housework. Like

Philopoemen he used to saw up our wood, doing everything with simplicity and dignity, for he seemed to realize that his objective added nobility to everything he did. When I left this good man to do my residence at the Hôtel Dieu, he felt an indescribable grief at the thought that he could no longer live with me. But he consoled himself with the prospect of saving up the money needed for the expenses of my thesis, and made me promise to come and see him on my days off. Bourgeat was proud of me; he loved me both for my sake and for his own. If you look up my thesis you will see that it was dedicated to him. During the last year of my internship, I had earned enough money to pay back everything I owed to this admirable Auvergnat, by buying him a horse and a water-cart. He was furious when he knew that I had been depriving myself of my money, and nevertheless he was delighted to see his wishes realized. He both laughed and scolded me. He looked at his cart and his horse, wiping a tear from his eyes as he said, "That's bad! Oh, what a splendid cart! You shouldn't have done it. The horse is as strong as an Auvergnat." I have never seen anything more moving than this scene. Bourgeat absolutely insisted on buying me that case of instruments mounted in silver which you have seen in my study, and which is for me the most valuable thing I have there. Although he was thrilled by my first successes, he never let slip the least word or gesture which implied, "That man's success is due to me." And yet, without him, poverty would have killed me. The poor man had dug his own grave to help me. He had eaten nothing but bread rubbed with garlic, so that I could have coffee to help me work at night. He fell ill. As you can imagine, I spent the nights at his bedside. I pulled him through the first time, but he had a relapse two years later, and in spite of the most constant care, in spite of the greatest efforts of medical science, his end had come. No king was ever as well cared for as he was. Yes, Bianchon, to snatch that life from death I made supreme efforts. I wanted to make him live long enough for me to show him the results of his work and realize all his hopes for me; I wanted to satisfy the only gratitude which has ever filled my heart and put out a fire which still burns me today.'

After a pause, Desplein, visibly moved, resumed his tale. 'Bourgeat, my second father, died in my arms leaving me everything he possessed in a will which he had had made by a public letter-writer and dated the year when we went to live in the Cour de Rohan. This man had the simple faith of a charcoal-burner. He loved the Blessed Virgin as he would have loved his wife. Although he was an ardent Catholic, he had never said a word to me about my lack of religion. When his life was in danger, he begged me to do everything possible to enable him to have the help of the Church. I had Mass said for him every day. Often, during the night, he would express fears for his future; he was afraid that he had not lived a sufficiently holy life. Poor man! He worked from morning to night. To whom then would Paradise belong – if there is a Paradise? He received the last rites like the saint he was and his death was worthy of his life. I was the only person to attend his funeral. When I had buried my only benefactor, I tried to think of a way of paying my debt to him. I realized that he had neither family nor friends, wife nor children. But he was a believer, he had a religious conviction. Had I any right to dispute it? He had spoken to me shyly about Masses said for the repose of the dead. He didn't want to impose this duty upon me, thinking that it would be like asking payment for his services. As soon as I could establish an endowment fund, I gave Saint-Sulpice the necessary amount to have four Masses said there a year. As the only thing I can give to Bourgeat is the satisfaction of his religious wishes, the day when this Mass is said at the beginning of each season, I say with the good faith of a doubter, "Oh God, if there is a sphere where, after their death, you place all those who have been perfect, think of good Bourgeat. And if there is anything for him to suffer, give me his sufferings so that he may enter more quickly into what is called Paradise." That, my dear fellow, is the most that a man with my opinions can allow himself. God must be a decent chap; he couldn't hold it against me. I swear to you, I would give my fortune to be a believer like Bourgeat.'

Bianchon, who looked after Desplein in his last illness, dares not affirm nowadays that the distinguished surgeon died an atheist. Believers will like to think that the humble Auvergnat will have opened the gate of heaven for him as, earlier, he had opened for him the gate of that earthly temple on whose doorway is written *Aux grands hommes la patrie reconnaissante*.

The Conscript

Sometimes they saw that, by a phenomenon of vision or movement, he could abolish space in its two aspects of Time and Distance, one of these being intellectual and the other physical. *Histoire Intellectuelle de Louis Lambert*.

One evening in the month of November 1793, the most important people in Carentan were gathered together in the drawing-room of Madame de Dey, who received company every day. Certain circumstances, which would not have attracted attention in a large town but which were bound to arouse curiosity in a small one, gave an unwonted interest to this everyday gathering. Two days earlier, Madame de Dey had closed her doors to visitors, and she had not received any the previous day either, pretending that she was unwell. In normal times these two events would have had the same effect in Carentan as the closing of the theatres has in Paris. On such days existence is, in a way, incomplete. But in 1793 Madame de Dey's behaviour could have the most disastrous consequences. At that time if an aristocrat risked the least step, he was nearly always involved in a matter of life and death. To understand properly the eager curiosity and the narrow-minded cunning which, during that evening, were expressed on the faces of all these Norman worthies, but above all to appreciate the secret worries of Madame de Dey, the part she played at Carentan must be explained. As the critical position in which she was placed at that time was, no doubt, that of many people during the Revolution, the sympathies of more than one reader will give an emotional background to this narrative.

Madame de Dey, the widow of a lieutenant-general, a chevalier of several orders, had left the Court at the beginning of the emigration. As she owned a considerable amount of property in the Carentan region, she had taken refuge there, hoping that the influence of the Terror would be little felt in those parts. This calculation, founded on an accurate knowledge of the region, was correct. The Revolution wrought little havoc in Lower Normandy. Although, in the past, when Madame de Dey visited her property in Normandy, she associated only with the noble families of the district, she now made a policy of opening her doors to the principal townspeople and to the new authorities, trying to make them proud of having won her over, without arousing either their hatred or their jealousy. She was charming and kind, and gifted with that indescribable gentleness which enabled her to please without having to lower herself or ask favours. She had succeeded in winning general esteem thanks to her perfect tact which enabled her to keep wisely to a narrow path, satisfying the demands of that mixed society without humiliating the touchy *amour propre* of the parvenus, or upsetting the sensibilities of her old friends.

She was about thirty-eight years old, and she still retained, not the fresh, rounded good looks which distinguish the girls of Lower Normandy, but a slender, as it were aristocratic, type of beauty. Her features were neat and delicate; her figure was graceful and slender. When she spoke, her pale face seemed to light up and come to life. Her large black eyes were full of friendliness, but their calm, religious expression seemed to show that the mainspring of her existence was no longer within herself. In the prime of her youth she had been married to a jealous old soldier, and her false position at a flirtatious court no doubt helped to spread a veil of serious melancholy over a face which must once have shone with the charms and vivacity of love. Since, at an age when a woman still feels rather than reflects, she had always had to repress her instinctive feminine feelings and emotions, passion had remained unawakened in the depths of her heart. And so her principal attraction stemmed from this inner youthfulness which was, at times, revealed in her face and which gave her thoughts an expression of innocent desire. Her appearance commanded respect, but in her bearing and in her voice there was always the expectancy of an unknown future as with a young girl. Soon after meeting her the least susceptible of men would find himself in love with her and yet retain a kind of respectful fear of her, inspired by her courteous, dignified manner. Her soul, naturally great but strengthened by cruel struggles, seemed far removed from ordinary humanity, and men recognized their inferiority. This soul needed a dominating passion. Madame de Dey's affections were thus concentrated in one single feeling, that of maternity. The happiness and the satisfactions of which she had been deprived as a wife, she found instead in the intense love she had for her son. She loved him not only with the pure and profound devotion of a mother, but with the coquetry of a mistress and the jealousy of a wife. She was unhappy when he was away, and, anxious during his absence, she could never see enough of him and lived only through and for him. To make the reader appreciate the strength of this feeling, it will suffice to add that this son was not only Madame de Dey's only child, but also her last surviving relative, the one being on whom she could fasten the fears, the hopes and the joys of her life. The late Comte de Dey was the last of his family and she was the sole heiress of hers. Material motives and interests thus combined with the noblest needs of the soul to intensify in the countess's heart a feeling which is already so strong in women. It was only by taking the greatest of care that she had managed to bring up her son and this had made him even more dear to her. Twenty times the doctors told her she would lose him, but confident in her own hopes and instincts, she had the inexpressible joy of seeing him safely overcome the perils of childhood, and of marvelling at the improvement in his health, in spite of the doctors' verdict.

Due to her constant care, this son had grown up and developed into such a charming young man that at the age of twenty he was regarded as one of the most accomplished young courtiers at Versailles. Above all, thanks to a good fortune which does not crown the efforts of every mother, she was adored by her son; they understood each other in fraternal sympathy. If they had not already been linked by the ties of nature, they would instinctively have felt for each other that mutual friendship which one meets so rarely in life. At the age of eighteen the young count had been appointed a sub-lieutenant of dragoons and in obedience to the code of honour of the period he had followed the princes when they emigrated.

Madame de Dey, noble, rich and the mother of an *émigré*, thus could not conceal from herself the dangers of her cruel situation. As her only wish was to preserve her large fortune for her son, she had denied herself the happiness of going with him, and when she read the strict laws under which the Republic was confiscating every day the property of *émigrés* at Carentan, she congratulated herself on this act of courage. Was she not watching over her son's wealth at the risk of her life? Then, when she heard of the terrible executions decreed by the Convention, she slept peacefully in the knowledge that her only treasure was in safety, far from the danger of the scaffold. She was happy in the belief that she had done what was best to save both her son and her fortune. To this private thought she made the concessions demanded by those unhappy times, without compromising her feminine dignity or her aristocratic convictions, but hiding her sorrows with a cold secrecy. She had understood the difficulties which awaited her at Carentan. To come there and occupy the first place, wasn't that a way of defying the scaffold every day? But, supported by the courage of a mother, she knew how to win the affection of the poor by relieving all kinds of distress without distinction, and made herself indispensable to the rich by ministering to their pleasures. She entertained at her house the *procureur* of the commune, the mayor, the president of the district, the public prosecutor and even the judges of the revolutionary tribunal. The first four of these were unmarried and so they courted her, hoping to marry her either by making her afraid of the harm they could do her or by offering her their protection. The public prosecutor, who had been *procureur* at Caen and used to look after the countess's business interests, tried to make her love him, by behaving with devotion and generosity – a dangerous form of cunning! He was the most formidable of all the suitors. As she had formerly been a client of his, he was the only one who had an intimate knowledge of the state of her considerable fortune. His passion was reinforced by all the desires of avarice and supported by an immense power, the power of life and death throughout the district. This man, who was still young, behaved with such an appearance of magnanimity that Madame de Dey had not yet been able to form an opinion of him. But, despising the danger which lay in vying in cunning with Normans, she made use of the inventive craftiness with which Nature has endowed women to play off these rivals against each other. By gaining time, she hoped to survive safe and sound to the end of the revolutionary troubles. At that period, the royalists who had stayed in France deluded themselves each day that the next day would see the end of the Revolution, and this conviction caused the ruin of many of them.

In spite of these difficulties, the countess had very skilfully maintained her independence until the day on which, with unaccountable imprudence, she took it into her head to close her door. The interest she aroused was so deep and genuine that the people who had come to her house that evening became extremely anxious when they learned that it was impossible for her to receive them. Then, with that frank curiosity which is engrained in provincial manners, they made inquiries about the misfortune, the sorrow, or the illness which Madame de Dey must be suffering from. An old servant named Brigitte answered these questions saying that her mistress had shut herself up in her room and wouldn't see anyone, not even the members of her own household. The almost cloister-like existence led by the inhabitants of a small town forms in them the habit of analysing and explaining the actions of others. This habit is naturally so invincible that after pitying Madame de Dey, and without knowing whether she was really happy or sad, everyone began to look for the causes of her sudden retreat.

'If she were ill,' said the first inquirer, 'she would have sent for the doctor. But the doctor spent the whole day at my house playing chess. He said to me jokingly that nowadays there is only one illness . . . and that unfortunately it is incurable.'

This jest was made with caution. Men and women, old men and girls then began to range over the vast field of conjectures. Each one thought he spied a secret, and this secret filled all their imaginations. The next day their suspicions had grown nastier. As life is lived in public in a small town, the women were the first to find out that Brigitte had bought more provisions than usual at the market. This fact could not be denied. Brigitte had been seen first thing in the morning in the market-square and – strange to relate – she had bought the only hare available. The whole town knew that Madame de Dey did not like game. The hare became a starting point for endless conjectures. As they took their daily walk, the old men noticed in the countess's house a kind of concentrated activity which was revealed by the very precautions taken by the servants to conceal it. The valet was beating a carpet in the garden. The previous day no one would have paid any attention to it, but this carpet became a piece of evidence in support of the fanciful tales which everyone was inventing. Each person had his own. The second day, when they heard that Madame de Dey said she was unwell, the leading inhabitants of Carentan gathered together in the evening at the mayor's brother's house. He was a retired merchant, married, honourable, generally respected, and the countess had a high regard for him. That evening all the suitors for the hand of the rich widow had a more or less probable tale to tell, and each one of them considered how to turn to his own profit the secret event which forced her to place herself in this compromising position. The public prosecutor imagined a whole drama in which Madame de Dey's son would be brought to her house at night. The mayor thought that a non-juring priest had arrived from La Vendée and sought asylum with her. But the purchase of a hare on a Friday couldn't be explained by this story. The president of the district was convinced that she was hiding a chouan or a Vendéen leader who was being hotly pursued. Others thought it was a noble who had escaped from the Paris prisons. In short, everyone suspected the countess of being guilty of one of those acts of generosity which the laws of that period called a crime and which could lead to the scaffold. The public prosecutor, however, whispered that they must be silent and try to save the unfortunate woman from the abyss towards which she was hastening.

'If you make this affair known,' he added, 'I shall be obliged to intervene, to search her house, and then! . . .' He said no more but everyone understood what he meant.

The countess's real friends were so alarmed for her that, on the morning of the third day, the *procureur-syndic* of the commune got his wife to write her a note urging her to receive company that evening as usual. Bolder still, the retired merchant called at Madame de Dey's house during the morning. Very conscious of the service which he wanted to render her, he insisted on being allowed in to see her, and was amazed when he caught sight of her in the garden, busy cutting the last flowers from her borders to fill her vases.

'She must have given refuge to her lover,' the old man said to himself, as he was overcome with pity for this charming woman. The strange expression of the countess's face confirmed his suspicions. The merchant was deeply moved by this devotion which is so natural to women, but which men always find touching because they are all flattered by the sacrifices which a woman makes for a man; he told the countess about the rumours which were all over the town, and of the danger in which she was placed. 'For,' he said in conclusion, 'though some of our officials may be willing to forgive you for acting heroically to save a priest, nobody will pity you if they find out you are sacrificing yourself for the sake of a love affair.'

At these words, Madame de Dey looked at the old man with a distraught and crazy expression which made him shudder, despite his age.

'Come with me,' she said taking him by the hand and leading him into her room where, having first made sure that they were alone, she took a dirty crumpled letter from the bodice of her dress. 'Read that,' she cried pronouncing the words with great effort.

She collapsed into her chair, as if she were overcome. While the old merchant was looking for his glasses and cleaning them, she looked up at him, examined him for the first time with interest and said gently in a faltering voice, 'I can trust you.'

'Have I not come to share in your crime?' replied the worthy man simply.

She gave a start. For the first time in this little town, her soul felt sympathy with another's. The merchant understood at once both the dejection and the joy of the countess. Her son had taken part in the Granville expedition; his letter to his mother was written from the depths of his prison, giving her one sad, yet joyful hope. He had no doubts about his means of escape, and he mentioned three days in the course of which he would come to her house, in disguise. The fatal letter contained heart-rending farewells in case he would not be at Carentan by the evening of the third day, and he begged his mother to give a fairly large sum of money to the messenger who, braving countless dangers, had undertaken to bring her this letter. The paper shook in the old man's hands.

'And this is the third day,' cried Madame de Dey as she got up quickly, took back the letter, and paced up and down the room.

'You have acted rashly,' said the merchant. 'Why did you have food brought in?'

'But he might arrive, dying with hunger, exhausted, and . . .' She said no more.

'I can count on my brother,' continued the old man, 'I will go and bring him over to your side.'

In this situation the merchant deployed again all the subtlety which he had formerly used in business and gave the countess prudent and wise advice. After they had agreed on what they both should say and do, the old man, on cleverly invented pretexts, went to the principal houses in Carentan. There he announced that he had just seen Madame de Dey, who would receive company that evening, although she was not very well.

As he was a good match for the cunning Norman minds who, in every family, cross-examined him about the nature of the countess's illness, he managed to deceive nearly everybody who was interested in this mysterious affair. His first visit worked wonders. He told a gouty old lady that Madame de Dey had nearly died from an attack of stomach gout. The famous Doctor Tronchin had on a former, similar occasion advised her to lay on her chest the skin of a hare, which had been flayed alive, and to stay absolutely immobile in bed. The countess who, two days ago, had been in mortal danger, was now, after having punctiliously obeyed Tronchin's extraordinary instructions, well enough to receive visitors that evening. This tale had an enormous success, and the Carentan doctor, a secret royalist, added to the effect by the seriousness with which he discussed the remedy. Nevertheless, suspicions had taken root too strongly in the minds of some obstinate people, or of some doubters, to be entirely dissipated. So, that evening, Madame de Dey's visitors came eagerly, in good time, some to observe her face carefully, others out of friendship, most of them amazed at her recovery. They found the countess by the large fireplace in her drawing-room, which was almost as small as the other drawing-rooms in Carentan, for to avoid offending the narrow-minded ideas of her guests, she had denied herself the luxuries she had been used to and so had made no changes in her house. The floor of the reception room was not even polished. She left dingy old hangings on the walls, kept the local furniture, burnt tallow candles and followed the fashions of the place. She adopted provincial life, without shrinking from its most uncomfortable meannesses or its most disagreeable privations. But, as

33

she knew that her guests would forgive her any lavishness conducive to their comfort, she left nothing undone which would minister to their personal pleasures. And so she always provided excellent dinners. She went as far as to feign meanness in order to please these calculating minds and she skilfully admitted to certain concessions to luxury, in order to give in gracefully. And so, about seven o'clock that evening, the best of Carentan's poor society was at Madame de Dey's house and formed a large circle around the hearth. The mistress of the house, supported in her trouble by the old merchant's sympathetic glances, endured with remarkable courage her guests' detailed questioning and their frivolous and stupid arguments. But at every knock on the door, and whenever there was a sound of footsteps in the street, she hid her violent emotion by raising questions of importance to the prosperity of the district. She started off lively discussions about the quality of the ciders and was so well supported by her confidant that the company almost forgot to spy on her, since the expression of her face was so natural and her self-possession so imperturbable. Nevertheless the public prosecutor and one of the judges of the revolutionary tribunal said little, watching carefully the least changes in her expression and, in spite of the noise, listening to every sound in the house. Every now and then they asked the countess awkward questions but she answered them with admirable presence of mind. A mother has so much courage! When Madame de Dey had arranged the card-players, and settled everyone at the tables to play boston or reversis or whist, she still lingered in quite a carefree manner to chat with some young people. She was playing her part like a consummate actress. She got someone to ask for lotto, pretended to be the only person who knew where the set was, and left the room.

'I feel stifled, my dear Brigitte,' she exclaimed as she wiped the tears springing from her eyes which shone with fever, grief and impatience. 'He is not coming,' she continued, as she went upstairs and looked round the bedroom. 'Here, I can breathe and live. Yet in a few more moments he will be here! For he is alive, of that I am sure. My heart tells me so. Don't you hear anything, Brigitte? Oh! I would give the rest of my life to know whether he is in prison or walking across the countryside. I wish I could stop thinking.'

She looked round the room again to see if everything was in order. A good fire was burning brightly in the grate, the shutters were tightly closed, the polished furniture was gleaming, the way the bed had been made showed that the countess had discussed the smallest details with Brigitte. Her hopes could be discerned in the fastidious care which had obviously been lavished on this room; in the scent of the flowers she had placed there could be sensed the gracious sweetness and the most chaste caresses of love. Only a mother could have anticipated a soldier's wants and made preparations which satisfied them so completely. A superb meal, choice wines, slippers, clean linen, in short everything that a weary traveller could need or desire was brought together so that he should lack for nothing, so that the delights of home should show him a mother's love.

'Brigitte,' cried the countess in a heart-rending voice as she went to place a chair at the table. It was as if she wanted to make her prayers come true, as if she wanted to add strength to her illusions.

'Ah, Madame, he will come. He is not far away — I am sure that he is alive and on his way. I put a key in the Bible and I kept it on my fingers while Cottin read the Gospel of St John . . . and, Madame, the key didn't turn.'

'Is that a reliable sign?' asked the countess.

'Oh, yes! Madame, it's well known. I would stake my soul he's still alive. God cannot be wrong.'

'I would love to see him, in spite of the danger he will be in when he gets here.'

'Poor Monsieur Auguste,' cried Brigitte, 'he must be on the way, on foot.'

'And there's the church clock striking eight,' exclaimed the countess in terror.

She was afraid that she had stayed longer than she should have done in this room where, as everything bore witness to her son's life, she could believe that he was still alive. She went downstairs but before going into the drawing-room, she paused for a moment under the pillars of the staircase, listening to hear if any sound disturbed the silent echoes of the town. She smiled at Brigitte's husband, who kept guard like a sentinel and seemed dazed with the effort of straining to hear the sounds of the night from the village square. She saw her son in everything and everywhere. She soon went back into the room, putting on an air of gaiety, and began to play lotto with some little girls. But every now and then she complained of not feeling well and sat down in her armchair by the fireplace.

That is how people and things were in Madame de Dey's house while on the road from Paris to Cherbourg a young man wearing a brown *carmagnole*, the obligatory dress of the period,

36

was making his way to Carentan. When the conscription of August 1793 first came into force, there was little or no discipline. The needs of the moment were such that the Republic could not equip its soldiers immediately, and it was not uncommon to see the roads full of conscripts still wearing their civilian clothes. These young men reached their halting places ahead of their battalions, or lagged behind, for their progress depended on their ability to endure the fatigues of a long march. The traveller in question was some way ahead of a column of conscripts which was going to Cherbourg and which the mayor of Carentan was expecting from hour to hour, intending to billet the men on the inhabitants. The young man was marching with a heavy tread, but he was still walking steadily and his bearing suggested that he had long been familiar with the hardships of military life. Although the meadow-land around Carentan was lit up by the moon, he had noticed big white clouds threatening a snowfall over the countryside. The fear of being caught in a storm probably made him walk faster, for he was going at a pace ill-suited to his fatigue. On his back he had an almost empty rucksack, and in his hand was a boxwood stick cut from one of the high, thick hedges which this shrub forms around most of the estates of Lower Normandy. A moment after the solitary traveller had caught sight of the towers of Carentan silhouetted in the eerie moonlight, he entered the town. His step aroused the echoes of the silent, deserted streets and he had to ask a weaver who was still at work the way to the mayor's house. This official did not live far away and the conscript soon found himself in the shelter of the porch of the mayor's house. He applied for a billeting order and sat down on

37

a stone seat to wait. But he had to appear before the mayor who had sent for him and he was subjected to a scrupulous cross-examination. The soldier was a young man of good appearance who seemed to belong to a good family. His demeanour indicated that he was of noble birth and his face expressed that intelligence which comes from a good education.

'What's your name?' asked the mayor looking at him knowingly.

'Julien Jussien,' replied the conscript.

'And where do you come from?' asked the official with an incredulous smile.

'From Paris.'

'Your comrades must be some distance away,' continued the Norman half jokingly.

'I am three miles ahead of the battalion.'

'Some special feeling attracts you to Carentan, no doubt, *citoyen réquisitionnaire*,' said the mayor shrewdly.

'It is all right,' he added, as with a gesture he imposed silence on the young man who was about to speak. 'We know where to send you. There you are,' he added giving him his billeting order. 'Off you go, *citoyen* Jussien.'

There was a tinge of irony in the official's tone as he pronounced these last two words and handed out a billet order giving the address of Madame de Dey's house. The young man read the address with an air of curiosity.

'He knows quite well that he hasn't far to go. And once he's outside he'll soon be across the square,' exclaimed the mayor talking to himself as the young man went out. 'He's got some nerve! May God guide him! He has an answer to everything.

Yes, but if anyone but me had asked to see his papers, he would have been lost.'

At this moment, the Carentan clocks had just struck half past nine. The torches were being lit in Madame de Dey's antechamber; the servants were helping their masters and mistresses to put on their clogs, their overcoats or their capes; the cardplayers had settled their accounts and they were all leaving together, according to the established custom in all little towns.

'It looks as if the prosecutor wants to stay,' said a lady, who noticed that this important personage was missing when, having exhausted all the formulae of leave-taking, they separated in the square to go to their respective homes.

In fact that terrible magistrate was alone with the countess who was waiting, trembling, till he chose to go.

After a long and rather frightening silence, he said at last, 'I am here to see that the laws of the Republic are obeyed . . .'

Madame de Dey shuddered.

'Have you nothing to reveal to me?' he asked.

'Nothing,' she replied, amazed.

'Ah, Madame,' cried the prosecutor sitting down beside her and changing his tone, 'at this moment, one word could send you or me to the scaffold. I have observed your character, your feelings, your ways too closely to share the mistake into which you managed to lead your guests this evening. I have no doubt at all that you are expecting your son.'

The countess made a gesture of denial, but she had grown pale and the muscles of her face had contracted under the necessity of assuming a false air of calmness.

'Well, receive him,' continued the magistrate of the Revolution, 'but don't let him stay under your roof after seven o'clock in the morning. At daybreak, tomorrow, I shall come to your house armed with a denunciation which I shall have drawn up . . .'

She looked at him with a dazed expression which would have melted the heart of a tiger.

He went on gently, 'I shall demonstrate the falsity of the denunciation by a minute search, and by the nature of my report you will be protected from all further suspicion. I shall speak of your patriotic gifts, of your civic devotion, and we shall all be saved.'

Madame de Dey was afraid of a trap. She stood there motionless but her face was burning and her tongue was frozen. The sound of the door-knocker rang through the house.

'Ah,' cried the terrified mother, falling on her knees. 'Save him, save him!'

'Yes, let us save him!' replied the public prosecutor, looking at her passionately, 'even at the cost of *our* lives.'

'I am lost,' she cried as the prosecutor politely helped her to rise.

'Ah! Madame,' he replied with a fine oratorical gesture, 'I want to owe you to nothing . . . but yourself.'

'Madame, he's –' cried Brigitte thinking her mistress was alone.

At the sight of the public prosecutor, the old servant who had been flushed with joy, became pale and motionless.

'Who is it, Brigitte?' asked the magistrate gently, with a knowing expression.

'A conscript sent by the mayor to be put up here,' replied the servant showing the billet order.

'That's right,' said the prosecutor after reading the order. 'A battalion is due in the town tonight.' And he went out.

At that moment the countess needed so much to believe in the sincerity of her former lawyer that she could not entertain the slightest doubt of it. Quickly she went upstairs, though she scarcely had the strength to stand. Then she opened her bedroom door, saw her son, and fell half-dead into his arms. 'Oh, my child, my child,' she cried sobbing and covering him with wild kisses.

'Madame,' said the stranger.

'Oh! It's someone else,' she cried. She recoiled in horror and stood in front of the conscript, gazing at him with a haggard look.

'Oh, good God, what a strong resemblance!' said Brigitte.

There was silence for a moment and even the stranger shuddered at the sight of Madame de Dey.

She leaned for support on Brigitte's husband and felt the full extent of her grief; this first blow had almost killed her. 'Monsieur,' she said, 'I cannot bear to see you any longer; I hope you won't mind if my servants take my place and look after you.'

She went down to her own room half carried by Brigitte and her old manservant.

'What, Madame!' cried the housekeeper as she helped her mistress to sit down. 'Is that man going to sleep in Monsieur Auguste's bed, put on Monsieur Auguste's slippers and eat the *pâté* that I made for Monsieur Auguste? If I were to be sent to the guillotine, I . . .'

41

'Brigitte,' cried Madame de Dey.

Brigitte said no more.

'Be quiet, you chatterbox,' said her husband in a low voice. 'You'll be the death of Madame.'

At this moment, the conscript made a noise in his room as he sat down to table.

'I can't stay here,' exclaimed Madame de Dey. 'I shall go into the conservatory. From there I shall be able to hear better what's going on outside during the night.'

She was still wavering between the fear of having lost her son and the hope of seeing him come back. The silence of the night was horrible. When the conscript battalion came into town and each man had to seek out his lodgings, it was a terrible time for the countess. Her hopes were dashed at every footstep, at every sound; then soon the awful stillness of Nature returned. Towards morning, the countess had to go back to her own room. Brigitte, who was watching her mistress's movements, did not see her come out; she went into the room and there found the countess dead.

'She must have heard the conscript finishing dressing and walking about in Monsieur Auguste's room singing their damned *Marseillaise*, as if he were in a stable,' cried Brigitte, 'That will have killed her!'

The countess's death was caused by a more important feeling and, very likely, by a terrible vision. At the exact moment when Madame de Dey was dying in Carentan, her son was being shot in Le Morbihan. We can add this tragic fact to all the observations that have been made of sympathies which override the laws of space. Some learned recluses, in their curiosity, have collected this evidence in documents which will one day serve as a foundation for a new science — a science that has hitherto failed to produce its man of genius.

The Purse

The hour when it is no longer day but night has not yet come is a delightful one for expansive temperaments. Then the glow of twilight casts its soft tints or its strange reflections over everything and encourages a reverie which blends vaguely with the play of light and shade. The silence which reigns nearly always at this moment endears it more especially to artists, who reflect, stand back from their work (which they can no longer continue) and pass judgement on it, intoxicating themselves with a theme whose inner meaning then suddenly flashes on the mind's eye of genius. Anyone who, lost in thought, has not lingered beside a friend during that moment of poetic reverie will find it difficult to understand its inexpressible benefits. In the half-light the physical tricks used by art to make things seem real disappear completely. If one is looking at a picture, the people represented seem both to speak and to walk; the shadow becomes real shadow, the daylight is real daylight, the flesh is alive, the eyes move, blood flows in the veins and fabrics glisten. The imagination helps every detail to appear natural and sees only the beauties of the work. At that hour illusion reigns supreme; perhaps it comes with the night? Is not illusion a kind of night for our thoughts, a night which we furnish with dreams? Illusion then spreads its wings, carries the soul away to the world of fantasies, a world rich in voluptuous and capricious desires, in which the artist forgets the real world, yesterday, tomorrow, and the future, even his troubles both good and bad.

At this magic hour, a talented young painter, who saw in art only art itself, was at the top of the double ladder that he was using to paint a large, high canvas, which was nearly completed. There, criticizing his work, admiring it in good faith, and following the drift of his thoughts, he was absorbed in one of those meditations which delight and exalt the soul, which charm and soothe it. His daydream must have lasted a long time. Night came. Whether he wanted to climb down the ladder or whether he made a false movement thinking he was on the floor, he could, in the circumstances, have no clear recollection of the causes of his accident. He fell, his head struck against a stool, he lost consciousness and lay motionless, for how long he did not know. A gentle voice roused him from the kind of daze in which he was sunk. When he opened his eyes the sight of a bright light made him shut them again quickly. But through the veil which shrouded his senses he heard two women whispering and felt two young, timid hands supporting his head. Soon he regained consciousness and, by the light of one of those old lamps with a double air-flow, he saw the most delightful girl's head that he had ever seen, one of those heads which are often taken for a fancy of the paintbrush. But for him this head suddenly made real the theories of ideal beauty which every artist creates for himself and which is the source of his talent. The unknown girl's face was of the fine-featured, delicate type, of the school of Proudhon's painting, as it were, and also had that poetic charm which Girodet gives to his imaginary faces. The smoothness of her brow, the regularity of her eyebrows, the purity of her features, the virginity clearly marked on her whole countenance, made of the girl a perfect creation. Her figure was lithe and slender, her curves were delicate. Her clothes, though simple and neat, indicated neither wealth nor poverty. As he returned to consciousness the painter expressed his admiration in a look of surprise, and stammered incoherent thanks. He found that his forehead was being pressed by a handkerchief and, in spite of the smell peculiar to studios, he recognized the strong smell of ether which must have been used to bring him round after his faint. Then, finally, he saw an old woman, who looked like a marchioness of the old régime, holding the lamp as she gave advice to the unknown girl.

'Monsieur,' replied the girl to one of the questions asked by the painter while his ideas were still in the state of confusion caused by the fall, 'my mother and I heard the noise of your fall on to the floor and we thought we could hear a groan. The silence which followed the fall frightened us and we hurried upstairs. We found the key in the door, fortunately took the liberty of coming in and found you stretched out motionless on the ground. My mother went to get everything needed to make a compress and revive you. You are hurt on the forehead, there. Do you feel it?'

'Yes, now I can,' he said.

'Oh, it's not serious,' added the old mother. 'Fortunately your head hit this dummy.'

'I feel a lot better,' replied the painter. 'I only need a carriage to take me home. The porter will get one for me.'

He wanted to repeat his thanks to the two strangers, but at every sentence the old lady interrupted him, saying, 'Tomorrow, Monsieur, be sure you apply leeches or have yourself bled.

Drink some glasses of cordial. Take care of yourself; falls are dangerous.'

The girl was looking furtively at the painter and at the pictures in the studio. Her expression and her glances were perfectly modest. Her curiosity seemed like absent-mindedness and her eyes appeared to express the interest which women, with gracious spontaneity, take in all our misfortunes. The two strangers seemed oblivious of the painter's works in the presence of the suffering artist. When he had reassured them about his condition, they left his room looking at him with a solicitude devoid of both exaggeration and familiarity; they asked no indiscreet questions and did not try to make him want to become acquainted with them. Their actions bore the mark of perfect simplicity and good taste. At first their noble, simple manners made little impression on the painter, but afterwards when he recalled all the circumstances of the accident, he was very much struck by them. As they came to the floor below the painter's studio, the old lady exclaimed gently, 'Adélaide, you left the door open.'

'That was to help me,' replied the painter with a grateful smile.

'Mother, you went downstairs just now,' replied the girl, blushing.

'Would you like us to go down with you?' the mother asked the painter. 'The staircase is dark.'

'No, thank you, Madame, I am much better.'

'Hold firmly on to the banisters!'

The two women stayed on the landing to give the young man a light, listening to the sound of his footsteps.

So that the reader can appreciate fully how piquant and unexpected this scene was for the painter, I must explain that he had only moved into his studio in the attic of this house a few days previously. The house was situated in the darkest and consequently the muddiest part of the Rue de Suresne, almost opposite the Madeleine church and two steps away from his flat in the Rue des Champs Elysées. As the fame which his talent had brought him had made him one of the most popular artists in France, he was beginning to be no longer in want and, as he put it, he was enjoying his last days of poverty. Instead of going to work in one of the studios on the outskirts of the city whose reasonable rent was proportionate to the modesty of his earnings, he had satisfied a desire which used to be renewed each day, avoiding a long journey and loss of time, now more valuable to him than ever. No one would have aroused more interest than Hippolyte Schinner if he had been willing to make himself known, but he did not lightly confide the secrets of his life. He was the idol of a poor mother who had brought him up at the cost of the most severe privations. Mademoiselle Schinner, the daughter of an Alsatian farmer, had never been married. Her tender heart had formerly been cruelly hurt by a rich man who did not pride himself on being very scrupulous in love affairs. As a young girl in all the flower of her beauty, in all the radiance of her life, at the expense of her heart and of her beautiful illusions, she suffered that disenchantment which comes so slowly and yet so quickly, for we want to put off believing in evil as long as possible, and yet it always seems to come too soon. The day of her disenchantment was a whole century of reflections and it also was a day of religious thoughts and resignation. She refused the help of the man who had deceived her, withdrew from society, and turned her fault into a triumph. She gave herself up entirely to maternal love, asking from it all its joys in return for the pleasures of social life to which she bade farewell. She supported herself by her own work, laying up a treasure in her son. And so, later on, one day, one hour repaid her for the long drawn-out sacrifices of her poverty. At the last exhibition her son had received the Cross of the Legion of Honour. The newspapers, unanimously in favour of an unknown talent, were still loud in their sincere praise. The artists themselves acknowledged Schinner as a master and the dealers covered his pictures with gold. At the age of twenty-five Hippolyte Schinner, to whom his mother had transmitted her womanly feelings, appreciated more than ever her situation in society. He wanted to restore to his mother the pleasures of which society had so long deprived her and so he lived for her, hoping by dint of fame and fortune to see her one day happy, rich, respected, surrounded by famous men. Schinner had accordingly selected his friends from amongst the most honourable and distinguished men. Discriminating in the choice of his social contacts he wanted to raise even higher the position which his talent had made so high already. Work, to which he had been dedicated since his youth, in forcing him to live in solitude (always the mother of great thoughts) had left him that splendid faith which is the ornament of the early years of life. His adolescent soul was not unaware of any of the thousand traits of modesty that make a young man a being apart, with a heart full of joys, of poetry, of virgin hopes which seem trivial to sophisticated people but which are deep because they are simple.

He had been gifted with those gentle, courteous manners which are so becoming and which attract even those who do not understand them. He was well built. His voice, which came from the heart, aroused noble feelings in others and, by a certain candour in its tone, indicated a genuine modesty. When you saw him you felt drawn towards him by one of those moral attractions which scientists fortunately cannot yet analyse. They would find in it some phenomenon of galvanism or the activity of some fluid or other and they would express our feelings in a formula of proportions of oxygen and electricity.

These details will perhaps enable self-assured people and well-dressed men to understand why, during the absence of the caretaker whom he had sent to the end of the Rue de la Madeleine to get a carriage, Hippolyte Schinner did not ask the porter's wife any questions about the two people whose kind hearts had been revealed to him. But although he replied with a 'yes' or a 'no' to the questions, quite natural in such a situation, which she asked him about his accident and the obliging intervention of the fourth-floor tenants, he could not prevent her from obeying her caretaker's instinct. She talked to him about the two strangers from her point of view and according to the below-stairs opinions of the porter's lodge.

'Oh,' she said, 'it must be Mademoiselle Leseigneur and her mother who have lived here for four years. We don't know yet what these ladies do. In the morning, only up to midday, an elderly half-deaf domestic help, who talks no more than a wall, comes to work for them. In the evenings, two or three old gentlemen, with decorations like yours, Monsieur, and one of them with a carriage, and servants and the reputation of having an income of sixty thousand livres, come to the ladies' flat and often stay very late. But they are very quiet tenants, like you, Monsieur. And they're economical too, they live on nothing; as soon as a bill comes, they pay it. It's odd, Monsieur. The mother has a different name from her daughter. Oh, when they go to the Tuileries, Mademoiselle is very splendid and she can't go out without being followed by young men. She very properly shuts the door in their faces. The landlord would never allow . . .'

The carriage had arrived, Hippolyte heard no more, and went home. His mother, to whom he told his adventure, dressed his injury again and did not allow him to go back to his studio the following day. The doctor was consulted, various remedies were ordered and Hippolyte stayed at home for three days. During this confinement his unoccupied imagination recalled vividly, as it were by fragments, the details of the scene which followed his fainting. The girl's profile stood out sharply from the haziness of his inner vision; he could see again the mother's worn face and still feel Adélaïde's hands. He observed again a gesture which he had not noticed much at first but whose perfect grace was brought out by memory. Then an attitude or the sound of a melodious voice, made more beautiful by the distance of memory, suddenly reappeared like objects which come to the surface after being dropped to the bottom of a pond. So, on the day when he was able to start work again, he went back to his studio early. But the visit which he was undeniably entitled to make to his neighbours was the real cause of his eagerness; he was already forgetting the pictures he had begun. At the moment when a passion breaks through its swaddling clothes there is an inexplicable pleasure which those who have loved will understand. Thus some people will know why the painter slowly climbed the stairs leading to the fourth floor and will share the secret of his rapid heartbeats when he saw the brown door of Mademoiselle Leseigneur's modest dwelling. This girl, who did not have the same name as her mother, had aroused a thousand sympathies in the young painter. He liked to think that he and she were in similar positions and he endowed her with the misfortunes of his own origin. As he worked Hippolyte yielded himself completely to thoughts of love and made a lot of noise in order to oblige the two ladies to think of him just as he was thinking of them. He stayed very late at his studio and had dinner there. Then about seven o'clock he went downstairs to his neighbours' flat.

Perhaps out of delicacy, no painter of social manners has dared to let us into the secrets of the really strange homes of some Parisians, those dwellings from which emerge such smart, such elegant toilettes, women who are so dazzling and appear so rich, yet in whose homes can be seen everywhere the signs of a shaky fortune. If the picture here is too bluntly portrayed, if you find it wearisome, do not blame the description, which is, as it were, an integral part of the story; for the appearance of his neighbours' flat had a strong influence on the feelings and hopes of Hippolyte Schinner.

The house belonged to one of those landlords who have a deep, built-in horror of repairs and improvements, one of those men who consider their position of Parisian landlord as a profession. In the great chain of moral types, these people are half-way between the miser and the money-lender. They are all calculating optimists and faithful to the *status quo* of Austria. If you talk of altering a cupboard or a door, of making the most essential ventilator, their eyes flash, their anger is aroused, they shy like frightened horses. When the wind has blown a few tiles off their chimneys they are ill, and deny themselves a visit to the Gymnase or the Porte-Saint-Martin because of the repairs. Hippolyte had had the free performance of a comic scene with milord Molineux in connection with certain improvements to be made in his studio, and so he was not surprised at the dark, greasy colours, at the oily streaks, at the stains and other rather disagreeable accessories which adorned the woodwork. These marks of poverty are not, moreover, without poetry in the eyes of an artist.

Mademoiselle Leseigneur came herself to open the door. She recognized the young painter and greeted him. Then, at the same time, with the dexterity of a Parisian and the presence of mind which comes from pride, she turned round to shut the door of a glazed partition. Through this door Hippolyte might have glimpsed some washing hung on lines above the economical stove, an old trestle bed, embers, coal, irons, the household filter, dishes and all the utensils peculiar to small households. Fairly clean muslin curtains carefully concealed this *capharnaüm* (a word used colloquially to indicate this kind of laboratory), which was moreover badly lit by apertures looking on to a neighbouring courtyard. With the quick glance of an artist, Hippolyte saw the function, the furniture, the general state of this first divided room. The respectable part, which served both as ante-room and as dining-room was papered with old, gold-coloured wallpaper with a velvet border, probably manufactured by Réveillon. Its holes and stains had been carefully concealed by wafers. Engravings by Lebrun representing Alexander's battles, but in frames with the gilt rubbed off, were hung symmetrically on the walls. In the middle of the room was a solid mahogany table of an old-fashioned shape and worn at the edges. A little stove, whose straight upright pipe was hardly visible, stood in front of the fireplace, and in the hearth was a cupboard. In strange contrast, the chairs showed traces of a past splendour; they were of carved mahogany. But the red leather of the seats, the gilded studs and the gold braid sported as many scars as the old sergeants of the Imperial Guard. The room served as a museum for certain things which are only found in this kind of ambiguous household, nameless objects partaking of both luxury and poverty. Amongst other curiosities Hippolyte noticed a magnificently decorated telescope hung above the little greenish mirror which adorned the chimney-piece. To match this strange furniture, there was, between the fireplace and the partition, a cheap sideboard painted to look like mahogany, of all woods the one that is the hardest to imitate. But the red, slippery tiled floor, the miserable little mats placed in front of the chairs, the furniture, everything shone with that polished cleanliness which lends a false lustre to old things by showing up even more their imperfections, their age and their long service. In the room there lingered an indefinable smell which came from the fumes of the *capharnaüm* mingled with the odours of the dining-room and the staircase, although the window was half open and the air from the street moved the cambric curtains. These were carefully draped so as to hide the recess where the previous tenants had left marks of their presence in several incrustations, like species of domestic frescoes. Adélaïde quickly opened the door of the other room into which she showed the painter with a certain pleasure. Hippolyte who, in the past, had seen the same signs of poverty in his mother's home, noticed them with the peculiarly vivid impression which characterizes our earliest memories, and appreciated better than anyone else would have done the details of this existence. In recognizing the kind of things that he had known in his childhood, the good-hearted young man had neither scorn for this concealed misfortune nor pride in the luxury which he had just won for his mother.

'Well, Monsieur, I hope you no longer feel the effects of your fall,' said the old mother getting up from an old-fashioned easy chair in the chimney corner and offering him an armchair.

'No, Madame. I have come to thank you for the good care you gave me and especially to thank Mademoiselle who heard me fall.'

As he said these words, marked by the adorable stupidity aroused in the mind by the first agitations of true love, Hippolyte looked at Adélaïde. The girl was lighting the lamp with the double air-flow, no doubt so that she could dispense with a candle standing in a large, flat brass candlestick and decorated with prominent ridges of wax because of excessive melting. She gave a slight nod, went to put the candlestick in the ante-room, and came back to put the lamp on the mantelpiece. She sat down near her mother, a little behind the painter, so that she could look at him comfortably while appearing to be very busy getting the lamp going; its light, dimmed by the damp of an unpolished chimney, was flickering as it struggled with a black, badly trimmed wick. On seeing the large mirror which decorated the chimney-piece, Hippolyte glanced at it quickly so that he could admire Adélaïde. The girl's little trick thus served only to embarrass both of them. As he chatted with Madame Leseigneur (for Hippolyte gave her that name on the off-chance) he examined the sitting-room, but discreetly and unobtrusively. The Egyptian faces of the iron fire-dogs could hardly be seen in the ash-filled hearth, in which two firebrands almost met in front of an artificial earthenware log buried as carefully as a miser's treasure. An old Aubusson carpet, well mended and much faded, threadbare as an old soldier's coat, left bare some of the tiled floor, whose chill could be felt. The walls were decorated with a reddish paper, imitating a figured silk material with yellow designs. In the middle of the wall opposite the windows the painter saw a crack and the chinks made in the wallpaper by the doors of a recess where presumably Madame Leseigneur slept and which was ill-concealed by a couch placed in front of it. Opposite the fireplace, above a mahogany chest decorated not without richness and taste, hung the portrait of a high-ranking officer which the painter could not see clearly in the dim light. But the little that he saw made him think that this frightful daub must have been painted in China. At the windows the red silk curtains were faded, as was the suite, upholstered with red and yellow tapestry, of this dual-purpose sitting-room. On the marble top of the chest was a valuable malachite tray, bearing a dozen magnificently painted coffee cups, probably made at Sèvres. On the mantelpiece was the ubiquitous Empire clock, a warrior guiding the four horses of a chariot with the number of an hour marked on each spoke of its wheel. The candles in the candelabra were yellowed with smoke and at each end of the mantelpiece could be seen a porcelain vase wreathed in artificial flowers, laden with dust and decorated with moss. In the middle of the room, Hippolyte noticed a card table set up and new cards. To an observer there was something indescribably sad in the sight of this poverty made up like an old woman who wants her face to belie her age. On seeing this room any sensible man would immediately have thought to himself: either these two women are the soul of honesty, or they live by scheming and gambling. But, looking at Adélaide, a young man as pure as Schinner was bound to believe in her perfect innocence and to ascribe to the most honourable causes the discrepancies of the furniture.

'Adélaide,' said the old lady to her daughter, 'I am cold. Make a little fire for us and give me my shawl.'

Adélaide went into a room next to the sitting-room, where presumably she slept, and came back bringing her mother a cashmere shawl which must have been very valuable when new (the patterns were Indian); but old, worn, and full of darns, it matched the furniture. Madame Leseigneur wrapped it round herself very artistically and with the skill of an old lady who wanted her words to be believed. The girl ran smartly to the *capharnaüm* and reappeared with a handful of sticks which she threw boldly on to the fire to relight it.

It would be quite difficult to reproduce the conversation which took place between these three people. Guided by the tact which nearly always comes from misfortunes experienced in childhood, Hippolyte did not dare to allow himself the slightest comment on his neighbours' circumstances as he saw around him the signs of such ill-concealed poverty. The simplest question would have been indiscreet and would have been permissible only in an old friend. Nevertheless, the painter was deeply affected by this concealed poverty, his generous soul was grieved by it. But as he knew how offensive any kind of pity, even the most friendly, can be, he was ill at ease because of the discrepancy between his thoughts and his words. The two ladies first of all talked about painting, for women are well aware of the hidden embarrassments occasioned by a first visit. Perhaps they experience these embarrassments themselves and their cast of mind provides a thousand ways of putting an end to them. As they asked the young man about the techniques of his art, about his studies, Adélaïde and her mother skilfully encouraged him to talk. The indefinable nothings of their kindly conversation naturally led Hippolyte to utter remarks or reflections which revealed his ways and his nature.

Sorrows had prematurely aged the old lady's face which had no doubt once been beautiful. But she retained only the prominent features, the outlines, in short the framework of a countenance which, taken as a whole, indicated great delicacy; there remained, too, considerable graciousness in the play of the eyes in which lay the indefinable expression peculiar to ladies of the old court. These fine, delicate features could just as well indicate evil feelings, suggest feminine wiles to a high degree of perversity, as reveal the sensitivity of a beautiful soul. Indeed a woman's face presents a problem to ordinary observers, for the difference between openness and deceit, between the gift for intrigue and the gift for genuine feeling is imperceptible. A man endowed with penetrating insight can guess at the intangible shades of meaning indicated by a line more or less curved, by a dimple more or less deep, by a feature more or less rounded or prominent. This kind of interpretation is dependent entirely on intuition, which alone can discover what everyone is concerned to hide. The old lady's face was like the flat she lived in. It seemed as difficult to know if this poverty concealed vices or great integrity as it was to tell whether Adélaide's mother was a former coquette in the habit of weighing up everything, calculating everything, selling everything, or an affectionate woman full of nobility and lovable virtues. But at Schinner's age, the first impulse of the heart is to believe in the good. And so, as he studied Adélaide's noble and almost haughty forehead, and looked at her expressive, thoughtful eyes, he inhaled, as it were, the sweet, modest scents of virtue. In the middle of the conversation, he took the opportunity of talking of portraits in general so that he would have an excuse for examining the frightful pastel drawing which had all its colours faded and its bloom largely worn away.

'Presumably you are attached to this picture because it resembles someone, Mesdames, for it's horribly ill drawn,' he said looking at Adélaide.

'It was done in Calcutta, in a great hurry,' replied the mother in a voice filled with emotion.

She looked at the clumsy sketch with that deep concentration aroused by reawakened happy memories which fall on the heart like a beneficent dew in whose fresh traces one gladly lingers. But in the expression of the old lady's face there were also signs of eternal mourning. This, at any rate, is how the painter interpreted his neighbour's demeanour and expression. Then he came and sat down beside her.

'Madame,' he said, 'in a little while the colours of this pastel drawing will have disappeared. The portrait will exist only in your memory. Where you will see a beloved face, others won't be able to see anything. Will you allow me to transfer this likeness to canvas? It will be more firmly fixed there than it is on this piece of paper. Since we are neighbours, give me the pleasure of doing this service for you. There are times when an artist likes to take a rest from his important compositions by doing less serious work, and so it will be a relaxation for me to repaint that head.'

The old lady gave a start when she heard these words, and Adélaïde gave the painter one of those thoughtful looks which seem to come straight from the heart. Hippolyte wanted to be linked with his neighbours by some kind of tie and to acquire the right to be part of their lives. His offer, which appealed to the keenest affections of their hearts, was the only one he could make. It satisfied his artist's pride and in no way offended the two ladies. Madame Leseigneur accepted the offer without being over-eager but with no reluctance, with the awareness of a fine soul that knows the extent of the bonds forged by such obligations and turns them into a token of great praise and esteem.

'Isn't that the uniform of a naval officer?' said the painter.

'Yes,' she said, 'it's the uniform of a ship's captain. Monsieur de Rouville, my husband, died in Batavia as the result of a wound received in a fight against an English ship which he encountered off the Asian coast. He commanded a frigate with fifty-six guns, and the *Revenge* was a ship with ninety-six. It was an unequal struggle but he defended himself so bravely that he fought till night came and he was able to escape. When I came back to France, Bonaparte wasn't yet in power and I was refused a pension. When, recently, I again asked for one the minister told me harshly that if Baron de Rouville had emigrated, he would still be alive, that he would probably have been a rear-admiral by now. Finally His Excellency ended by citing against me some law or other about the forfeiture of rights. I took this step, which friends urged me to take, only for the sake of my poor Adélaïde. I have always disliked holding out my hand in the name of a grief which deprives a woman of her voice and her strength. I don't like this pecuniary evaluation of blood which has been irreparably spilt.'

'Mother, this topic of conversation always upsets you.'

At Adélaïde's words, the Baronne Leseigneur de Rouville bowed her head and said no more.

'Monsieur,' said the girl to Hippolyte, 'I thought that painters' work didn't usually make a lot of noise?'

At this question, Schinner began to blush remembering the din he had made. Adélaïde said no more and saved him from telling a lie by suddenly getting up at the sound of a carriage stopping at the door. She went into her room, from which she immediately returned with two gilded candlesticks containing half-used candles which she lit straight away. And without waiting for the ring at the bell, she opened the door of the first room where she left the lamp. The sound of a kiss being given and received went straight to Hippolyte's heart. The young

61

man's impatience to see the person who was on such familiar terms with Adélaide was not satisfied immediately, for, speaking in low tones, the new arrivals had a conversation with her which he found very long. At last, Mademoiselle de Rouville reappeared followed by two men whose clothes, faces and appearance are in themselves a whole story.

The first one, aged about sixty, was wearing one of those jackets invented, I think, for Louis XVIII, who was then on the throne. By means of these jackets, a tailor, who ought to be immortalized, solved the most difficult sartorial problem. That artist certainly knew the art of compromise, an art which was the whole spirit of that politically mobile period. Is it not quite a rare merit to be able to judge one's own period? This coat, that the young men of today might take as legendary, was neither civilian nor military and could in turn pass for either. Embroidered fleurs-de-lis decorated the facings of the two coat-tails at the back. There were also fleurs-de-lis on the gilt buttons. On the shoulders two empty loops were crying out for useless epaulettes. These two military indications were there like a petition without a recommendation. In the buttonhole of the old man's royal blue cloth coat was a rosette made of several ribbons. He presumably always carried in his hand his three-cornered hat decorated with gold braid, for the snow-white tufts of his powdered hair showed no trace of pressure from the hat. He looked as if he was not more than fifty and seemed to enjoy robust health. While revealing the loyal, frank character of the old *émigrés* his face also indicated the free-thinking, easy-going ways, the gay passions and light-heartedness of those musketeers who used to be so famous in the annals of gallantry.

His gestures, his gait, his manners proclaimed that he was not willing to amend his royalism, his religion or his love affairs.

A truly fantastic figure followed this pretentious *voltigeur de Louis XIV* (that was the nickname given by the Bonapartists to these noble remnants of the monarchy). But to describe him properly I would need to make him the central figure of the picture where he is only an accessory. Imagine a thin, dried-up person, dressed like the first one, but as it were only his reflection, or if you like, his shadow. The one had a new coat, the other's was old and shabby. The hair powder of the second man seemed less white, the gold of the fleurs-de-lis less brilliant, the epaulette loops more disconsolate and more crumpled, the intelligence weaker, the life more advanced towards its fatal ending than the first man's. In short he embodied Rivarol's remark about Champcenetz: 'He is my moonlight.' He was only the double of the other, a pale, poor double, for between them there was all the difference that exists between the first and last print of a lithograph. This silent old man was a mystery to the painter and always remained so. The chevalier (for he was a chevalier) did not speak and no one spoke to him. Was he a friend, a poor relation, a man who stayed with the old lady-killer like a paid companion with an old lady? Was he a cross between a dog, a parrot and a friend? Had he saved his benefactor's fortune or only his life? Was he the Trim of another Captain Toby? Elsewhere, just as at the Baronne de Rouville's, he always aroused curiosity without ever satisfying it. During the Restoration, who could remember the attachment which before the Revolution had bound this chevalier to his friend's wife, dead for twenty years?

The person who appeared to be the freshest of these two remnants went gallantly up to the Baronne de Rouville, kissed her hand, and sat down beside her. The other bowed and placed himself close to his model at two chairs' distance. Adélaide came and leaned her elbows on the back of the armchair occupied by the old nobleman, imitating, without realizing it, the pose which Guérin gave to Dido's sister in his famous painting. Although the familiarity with which the nobleman treated her was that of a father, for the moment his liberties seemed to displease the girl.

'Well, you are sulking!' he said. Then he gave Schinner one of those subtle, crafty side glances which diplomatically express the prudent concern, the polite curiosity of well-bred people who, on seeing a stranger, seem to ask, 'Is he one of us?'

'This is our neighbour,' the old lady said to him, indicating Hippolyte. 'Monsieur is a famous painter whose name you must know despite your lack of interest in the arts.'

The nobleman appreciated the old lady's trick in not mentioning the name and bowed to the young man.

'Indeed,' he said, 'I heard a lot about his pictures at the last Salon. Talent has great privileges, Monsieur,' he added looking at the artist's red ribbon. 'The distinction which we must earn at the cost of our blood and of long service, you artists obtain it young. But all men of renown are brothers,' he added touching his Saint-Louis Cross.

Hippolyte stammered a few words of thanks and then became silent again, content to admire with increasing enthusiasm the beautiful girl's head, which delighted him. He soon forgot himself as he gazed at her, thinking no more of the great

64

poverty of the house. For him, Adélaïde's face stood out against a halo of light. He replied briefly to the questions addressed to him; fortunately he heard them, thanks to our peculiar intellectual faculty of sometimes being able, in a way, to think of two things at once. Who has not been lost in a joyful or sad meditation and listened to its inner voice, and at the same time taken part in a conversation or attended to someone reading aloud? Admirable duality which often helps us to be patient with bores! Hope, smiling and full of promise, inspired him with a thousand thoughts of future happiness, and he no longer paid any attention to his surroundings. He was a trusting youth and felt that it was shameful to analyse a pleasure.

After a certain time he noticed that the old lady and her daughter were playing cards with the old nobleman. As for the latter's satellite, faithful to his role of shadow, he stood behind his friend, absorbed in his game, replying to the player's unspoken questions with little approving grimaces which reproduced the questioning movements of the other man's face.

'Du Halga, I always lose,' said the nobleman.

'You discard badly,' replied the Baronne de Rouville.

'For three months now I haven't been able to win a single game from you,' he continued.

'Have you the aces, Monsieur le Comte?' asked the old lady.

'Yes. One more doomed,' he said.

'Would you like my advice?' asked Adélaïde.

'No, no, stay in front of me. The devil! It would be losing too much not to have you opposite me.'

At last the game ended. The nobleman took out his purse and, as he threw two louis on to the card table, he said, not without irritation, 'Forty francs, as right as gold. And deuce, it's eleven o'clock.'

'It's eleven o'clock,' repeated the silent character looking at the painter.

The young man, hearing these words a little more clearly than all the others, thought that it was time to take his leave. Then, coming back to the everyday world, he thought up some conventional words of conversation, bowed to the baroness, her daughter and the two strangers and left the room a prey to the first delights of true love, and without trying to analyse the unimportant events of the evening.

The next day the young painter felt a violent desire to see Adélaïde again. If he had listened to his passion, he would have gone to visit his neighbours again at six o'clock in the morning on arriving at his studio. He had enough rationality, however, to wait until the afternoon. But as soon as he thought he could call on Madame de Rouville, he went downstairs and rang the bell, not without some wild beatings of the heart. Blushing like a girl, he shyly asked Mademoiselle Leseigneur, who had come to open the door, for the Baron de Rouville's portrait.

'Do come in,' said Adélaïde, who had no doubt heard him coming down from his studio.

The painter followed her. He was embarrassed, abashed, not knowing what to say, so stupid had happiness made him. To see Adélaïde, to hear the rustle of her dress after having wanted for a whole morning to be near her, after having got up a hundred times, saying, 'I am going downstairs!' and not to have gone downstairs, this for him was to live so fully that if these feelings had been prolonged for too long they would have worn out his soul. The heart has the strange power of setting an extraordinary value on trifles. What a delight it is for a traveller to pick a blade of grass or an unknown leaf if he has risked his life in looking for it! The trifles of love are like this.

The old lady was not in the sitting-room. Adélaide, finding herself alone with the painter, brought a chair so that she could reach the portrait. But when she saw that she could not take it down without standing on the chest, she turned to Hippolyte and said, blushing, 'I am not tall enough. Will you get it?'

A feeling of modesty, revealed in the expression of her face and the tone of her voice, was the true motive for her request, and the young man, appreciating this, gave her one of those understanding looks which are love's sweetest language. On seeing that the painter had guessed her thoughts, Adélaide lowered her eyes with a movement of virginal pride. Then, since he could think of nothing to say and was almost in awe of her, the painter took down the picture, examined it gravely in the light near the window and went away without saying anything to Mademoiselle Leseigneur but 'I'll bring it back soon.' During this fleeting moment both of them experienced one of those sharp emotional shocks whose effects on the soul can be likened to those produced by a stone thrown to the bottom of a lake. The sweetest thoughts arise in quick succession, indefinable, manifold, aimless, disturbing the heart like the rings which, starting from the spot where the stone fell, make ripples in the water for a long time. Hippolyte went back to his studio armed with the portrait. Already a canvas had been fixed on his easel, a palette had been filled with colours. The paint-brushes had been cleaned, and the position and lighting selected. And so till dinner time, he worked at the portrait with the ardour that artists devote to their whims. He returned the same evening to the Baronne de Rouville's and stayed there from nine o'clock till eleven. Apart from the different subjects of conversation, this evening was exactly like the previous one. The two old men came at the same time, they played the same game of piquet, the players made the same remarks, and Adélaide's admirer lost as large a sum of money as he had done the evening before. Only Hippolyte was a little bolder and dared to talk to Adélaide.

A week went by like this, a week in which the painter's and Adélaide's feelings underwent those delightful, slow changes which lead hearts to a complete understanding of each other. So, day by day, the look with which Adélaide greeted her friend became more intimate, more trusting, more gay and frank, her voice and manners became less restrained and more familiar. Schinner wanted to learn piquet. As he was ignorant and new to the game he naturally had to be taught again and again, and, like the old man, he lost nearly every game. Although they had not yet confided their love to each other the two lovers knew that they belonged to each other. Both of them laughed, chatted, exchanged their thoughts, and spoke about themselves with the naïveté of two children who, in the space of a day, have become as well acquainted as if they had known each other for three years. Hippolyte enjoyed exercising his power over his shy sweetheart. Adélaide made many concessions to him. Timid and devoted, she was taken in by those pretended sulks which the least skilful lover or the most naïve girl invents and makes use of continually, just as spoilt children take advantage of the power given them by their mother's love. So there was a sudden end to all intimacy between the old count and Adélaide. From the sharp tone of the few words Hippolyte uttered whenever the old man unceremoniously kissed her hands or neck, she understood the painter's distress and the thoughts concealed beneath his frowning brow. On her side Mademoiselle Leseigneur soon asked her lover for a strict account of his slightest actions. She was so unhappy, so anxious when Hippolyte did not come. She knew so well how to scold him for his absences that the painter had to give up seeing his friends and going into society. Adélaide showed a woman's natural jealousy when she learned that sometimes, on leaving Madame de Rouville's, the painter paid further visits and frequented the most brilliant salons of Paris. According to her, this kind of life was bad for the health. Then, with that deep conviction to which the voice, gesture and look of a loved one give so much weight, she claimed that 'a man who is obliged to lavish his title and the charms of his intelligence on several women at once could not be the object of a very keen affection'. So the painter was led as much by the tyranny of his passion as by the demands of a girl in love, to live only in this little flat where everything pleased him. In short, no love was ever more pure or ardent. On both sides, the same faith, the same delicacy made their passion grow without the help of the sacrifices with which many people seek to prove their love. There existed between them a continual interchange of such sweet feelings that they did not know which of the two gave or received more. An involuntary inclination made the union of their two hearts ever closer. The progress of this genuine feeling was so rapid that, two months after the accident to which the painter owed the happiness of knowing Adélaide, their lives had become one. First thing in the morning, as she heard the painter's step, the girl could say to herself, 'He is there!' When Hippolyte went home to his mother's at dinner time, he never failed to look in on his neighbours. And in the evening he hurried there at the usual time with the punctuality of a man in love. Thus the most tyrannical woman, the most ambitious in love, could not have made the slightest reproach to the young painter. Adélaide therefore enjoyed an unmixed and unlimited happiness as she saw the full realization of the ideal which it is so natural to dream of at her age. The old nobleman came less often. The jealous Hippolyte had replaced him in the evenings at the green card table, in his perpetual bad luck at cards. Yet, in the midst of his happiness, a troublesome idea struck him as he thought of Madame de Rouville's terrible situation, for he had had more than one proof of her poverty. Several times already he had said to himself as he went home, 'What, twenty francs every evening?' And he did not dare admit to himself horrible suspicions. He took two months to paint the portrait, and when it was finished, varnished, and framed he looked on it as one of his best works. The Baronne de Rouville had said nothing more to him about it. Was this because of lack of concern or pride? The painter did not try to explain her silence.

He conspired happily with Adélaide to put the portrait in its place in Madame de Rouville's absence. So one day, while her mother was taking her usual walk in the Tuileries gardens, Adélaide, for the first time, went upstairs alone to Hippolyte's studio, under the pretext of seeing the portrait in the favourable light in which it had been painted. She remained silent and motionless, a prey to a delightful meditation in which all her womanly feelings were fused into one. Were they not all summed up in admiration for the man she loved? When the painter, uneasy at this silence, turned to look at her, she held out her hand to him, unable to say a word. But two tears had fallen from her eyes. Hippolyte took her hand and covered it with kisses. For a moment they looked at each other in silence, both wanting to confess their love and not daring to. The painter kept Adélaïde's hand in his. The same warmth and the same agitation told them then that their hearts were beating equally strongly. Overcome with emotion, the girl gently drew away from Hippolyte and said, looking at him ingenuously, 'You will make my mother very happy.'

'What, only your mother?' he asked.

'Oh! I am too happy already.'

The painter bowed his head and said no more, frightened by the violence of the feelings which the tone of these words awoke in his heart. Then, as they both understood the danger of the situation, they went downstairs and hung the portrait in its place. For the first time, Hippolyte dined with the baroness who, in her emotion and all in tears, wanted to kiss him. In the evening, the old _émigré_, the former comrade of the Baron de Rouville, paid a visit to his two friends to inform them that he had just been appointed vice-admiral. His navigations by land across Germany and Russia had been counted in his favour as naval campaigns. At the sight of the portrait, he cordially shook the painter's hand and exclaimed, 'Faith! Although my old carcass isn't worth the trouble of preserving, I would gladly give five hundred pistoles to see as good a likeness of myself as my old friend Rouville's.'

At this suggestion, the baroness looked at her friend and smiled, while signs of a sudden gratitude lit up her face. Hippolyte had the impression that the old admiral wanted to give him the price of the two portraits in paying for his own. His artist's pride, perhaps, as much as his jealousy, took offence at this thought and he replied, 'Monsieur, if I were a portrait painter, I wouldn't have painted this one.'

The admiral bit his lips and began to play. The painter stayed beside Adélaide, who suggested six points at piquet. He accepted. As he played, he noticed that Madame de Rouville had a zeal for the game that surprised him. Never before had the old baroness shown such an ardent desire to win, nor such a keen pleasure as she handled the nobleman's gold coins. During the evening, evil suspicions disturbed Hippolyte's happiness and made him distrustful. Could it be that Madame de Rouville lived by gambling? Was she not playing just now in order to pay a debt, or egged on by some necessity? Perhaps she hadn't paid her rent? The old man seemed shrewd enough not to let his money be taken with impunity. What interest attracted him, a rich man, to this poor house? Why, when he had formerly been so familiar with Adélaide, had he given up the liberties he had acquired and which perhaps were due to him? These involuntary reflections stimulated him to look carefully at the old man and the baroness whose looks of mutual understanding and side glances at Adélaide and himself displeased him. 'Could it be that they are deceiving me?' was Hippolyte's final, horrible, degrading thought, in which he believed just enough to be tortured by it. He wanted to stay after the old man's departure so that he could confirm or refute his suspicions. He took out his purse to pay Adélaide. But, carried away by his agonizing thoughts, he put it on the table and fell into a reverie which did not last long. Then, ashamed of his silence, he got up, replied to a conventional question asked by Madame de Rouville and went up to her so that, as he talked, he could examine her old face more carefully. He left the house, a prey to a thousand doubts. After going down a few steps, he went back to pick up his forgotten purse.

'I left my purse with you,' he said to Adélaide.

'No,' she replied, blushing.

'I thought it was there,' he added, pointing to the card table. He was ashamed for the baroness and for Adélaide that he did not see it there. He gave them a dazed look which made them laugh, turned pale and said as he felt his waistcoat, 'I've made a mistake, I've probably got it.'

In one of the compartments of that purse were fifteen louis and, in the other, some small change. The theft was so flagrant, so shamelessly denied, that Hippolyte no longer doubted his neighbours' immorality. He stopped on the stairs, and went down with difficulty. His legs were trembling, he was dizzy, he was perspiring, he was shivering and he found that he was not in a fit state to walk; he was struggling with the terrible emotion caused by the reversal of all his hopes. Then he dragged up from his memory a host of things he had noticed, apparently slight, but which corroborated his frightful suspicions and which, proving the reality of this final deed, opened his eyes to the character and way of life of these two women. Had they waited to steal the purse until the portrait had been delivered? Premeditated, the theft seemed even more loathsome. To add to his misery, the painter remembered that for two or three evenings, Adélaïde, who, with the curiosity of a young girl, appeared to be examining the particular kind of needlework of the worn-out silk web, was probably checking the amount of money in the purse. She seemed to be teasing innocently as she did so, but her aim was probably to watch for the moment when the amount would be big enough to be worth stealing. 'Perhaps the old admiral has very good reasons for not marrying Adélaïde, and then the baroness will have tried to . . .'

At this supposition, he stopped, not even finishing his thought which was contradicted by a very sensible reflection. 'If the baroness,' he thought, 'hopes to marry me to her daughter, they would not have robbed me.' Then, in order not to give up his illusions and his love, which was already so deeply rooted, he tried to explain his loss by blaming it on chance. 'My purse must have fallen on the floor,' he said to himself, 'it must have been left on my armchair. Perhaps I still have it, I am so absent-minded.' He searched himself quickly but did not find the accursed purse. His memory cruelly recalled the fatal truth, moment by moment. He could distinctly see his purse, lying on the top of the table but, since he had no more doubts about the theft, he then made excuses for Adélaïde, telling himself that one should not judge the unfortunate so hastily. There was no doubt some secret behind this deed which seemed so degrading. He did not want her proud and noble figure to prove false. Nevertheless the poverty-stricken flat seemed to him devoid of the poetry of love which beautifies everything. He saw it as dirty and shabby, and looked on it as the outward sign of an inner life which was ignoble, idle and vicious. Are not our feelings, as it were, inscribed on the things around us?

The next morning, he got up after a sleepless night. Heartache, that serious moral illness, had made enormous progress within him. To lose a happiness that had been dreamed of, to give up a whole future is a more acute suffering than that caused by the collapse of an experienced happiness, however complete it may have been. Is not hope better than memory? The meditations into which our minds suddenly fall are then like a sea without a shore, in whose depths we can swim for a moment but where our love must drown and perish. And it is a terrible death. Are not feelings the most brilliant part of our lives? In certain constitutions, delicate or strong, this partial death brings about the great ravages caused by disillusions, by unfulfilled hopes and passions. That was the case with the young painter. He left the house early and went for a walk in the cool shade of the Tuileries gardens, lost in his thoughts, forgetting everything in the world. There he happened to meet one of his closest friends, a school and studio companion with whom he had lived on better terms than one does with a brother.

'Well, Hippolyte, what's the matter?' asked François Souchet, a young sculptor who had just won the *grand prix* and was soon to go off to Italy.

'I am very unhappy,' replied Hippolyte seriously.

'Only an affair of the heart can upset you. Money, fame, esteem, you have everything.'

Gradually, the painter began to pour out his heart and confessed his love. As soon as he mentioned the Rue de Suresne and a young lady living on a fourth floor, Souchet cried cheerfully, 'Stop. She's a little girl whom I see every morning at the Assumption and whom I am courting. But, my dear fellow, we all know her. Her mother is a baroness. Do you believe in baronesses who live on the fourth floor? Brrr. Ah well, you are a man of the Golden Age. We see the old mother here, on this path, every day. But she's got a face, an appearance which tell the whole story. What, you haven't guessed what she is from the way she holds her bag?'

The two friends walked for a long time and were joined by several young men who knew Souchet or Schinner. The sculptor, thinking it not very serious, told them about the painter's experience.

'He's seen that little girl too,' he said.

There were comments and laughs and innocent teasing of the jocular kind usual with artists, but which made Hippolyte suffer terribly. A certain inner delicacy made him feel ill at ease at seeing his heart's secret treated so lightly, his passion rent apart and torn to shreds, and an unknown young girl whose face seemed so modest, subjected to true or false judgements made so thoughtlessly. He pretended to be moved by a spirit of contradiction. He seriously asked each of his companions for proofs of their assertions and the teasing started again.

'But, my dear fellow, have you seen the baroness's shawl?' asked Souchet.

'Have you followed the little girl when she trips along to the Assumption in the morning?' said Joseph Bridau, a young art student from Gros' studio.

'Oh, amongst other virtues, the mother has a certain grey dress which I regard as a model,' said Bixiou, the caricaturist.

'Listen, Hippolyte,' continued the sculptor, 'come here about four o'clock and just analyse the way the mother and daughter walk. If you still have doubts after that, well, we'll never be able to do anything with you. You will be capable of marrying your caretaker's daughter.'

A prey to the most conflicting feelings, the painter left his friends. It seemed to him that Adélaïde and her mother must be above these accusations and in his innermost heart he felt remorse at having suspected the purity of this beautiful, unsophisticated girl. He went back to his studio, passed by the door of the flat where Adélaïde lived and felt a pang which no man could mistake. He was so passionately in love with Mademoiselle de Rouville that, in spite of the theft of the purse, he still adored her. His love was like that of the Chevalier des Grieux who admired and purified his mistress even when she was on the cart which takes fallen women to prison. 'Why should not my love make her the purest of all women? Why abandon her to vice and evil without holding out a friendly hand?' He liked the idea of such a mission. Love turns everything to its advantage. Nothing attracts a young man more than to play the part of a good genius to a woman. There is something indescribably romantic about such an undertaking which suits passionate hearts. Is this not extreme devotion in its noblest and most gracious form? Is there not some greatness in knowing that you are so much in love that you still love when other people's love fades away and dies? Hippolyte sat down in his studio, looked at his picture without working at it, seeing the figures only through the tears which were swimming in his eyes, keeping his brush in his hand, and going up to the canvas as if to soften a colour, and not touching it. He was still in this state when night overtook him. The darkness aroused him from his meditation. He went downstairs, met the old admiral on the staircase, gave him a grim look as he greeted him and fled. He had meant to call on his neighbours, but the sight of Adélaide's protector froze his heart and made his resolution melt away. He wondered for the hundredth time what motive could bring the old lady-killer, a rich man with an income of eighty thousand livres, to this fourth floor where every evening he lost about forty francs; and he thought he could guess what that motive was. The next day and the following days, Hippolyte threw himself into his work and tried to fight against his passion with the enthusiasm of his ideas and the energy of his creative imagination. He half succeeded. Work consoled him, yet without managing to stifle the memories of so many affectionate hours spent with Adélaide.

One evening, as he left his studio, he found the door of the two ladies' flat half open. There was someone standing there in the window bay. Owing to the situation of the staircase and the door the painter could not pass by without seeing Adélaide. He bowed to her coldly giving her a glance loaded with indifference. But estimating the girl's sufferings by the extent of his own, he had an inner pang as he thought of the bitter grief which such a look and such coldness must arouse in a loving heart. To crown the sweetest joys that have ever delighted two pure hearts with a week's disdain and with the deepest and most utter contempt ... what a frightful conclusion! Perhaps the purse had been found again, and perhaps Adélaide had waited every evening for her sweetheart. This simple, natural thought aroused further remorse in the lover. He asked himself if the affection which the girl had showed him, if the delightful conversations imbued with a love which had charmed him, did not deserve at least an inquiry, were not worth an attempt at justification. Ashamed at having resisted his heart's desires for a whole week, and considering that this struggle was almost criminal, he went that same evening to Madame de Rouville's. All his suspicions, all his evil thoughts vanished at the sight of Adélaide, who had turned pale and thin.

'My goodness, what's the matter with you?' he said after greeting the baroness.

Adélaide made no reply but gave him a look filled with melancholy, a sad, discouraged look which pained him.

'You have no doubt been working hard,' said the old lady. 'You have changed. It is because of us that you have shut yourself away. The portrait must have delayed some pictures which are important for your reputation.'

Hippolyte was happy to find such a good excuse for his discourtesy.

'Yes,' he said, 'I have been very busy, but I have suffered . . .'

At these words, Adélaide raised her head, looked at her lover and her anxious eyes ceased to reproach him.

'So you thought we were quite indifferent to what good or bad fortune might befall you?' asked the old lady.

'I was wrong,' he replied. 'Yet there are troubles that one can't confide to just anyone, even to friendships of longer standing than that with which you honour me.'

'The sincerity and strength of a friendship should not be measured according to time. I have seen old friends not shed a tear for each other in misfortune,' said the baroness shaking her head.

'But what's the matter?' the young man asked Adélaide.

'Oh, nothing,' the baroness replied. 'Adélaide has had some late nights finishing a piece of needlework and wouldn't listen to me when I told her that a day more or less mattered little.'

Hippolyte was not listening. When he saw these two calm, noble faces, he blushed at his suspicions, and attributed the loss of his purse to some unknown accident. The evening was delightful for him and perhaps for her too. There are secrets which young hearts understand so well. Adélaide guessed Hippolyte's thoughts. Without being willing to confess his errors, the painter acknowledged them. He returned to his mistress more loving, and more affectionate, trying in this way to buy himself a tacit pardon. Adélaide experienced such perfect, such sweet happiness, that she felt as if all the distress which had so cruelly hurt her was not too high a price to pay for it. Nevertheless, the genuine harmony of their hearts, this understanding full of a magic charm, was disturbed by a phrase of the Baronne de Rouville's.

'Shall we have our little game?' she asked; 'for my old friend Kergarouet is annoyed with me.'

This remark aroused all the young painter's fears. He blushed as he looked at Adélaide's mother, but he saw on her face only the expression of an honest good nature. No hidden thought destroyed its charm, its delicacy was not treacherous, its irony was gentle and no remorse disturbed its calm. So he sat down at the card table. Adélaide wanted to share the painter's hand, claiming that he didn't know piquet and needed a partner. During the game Madame de Rouville and her daughter exchanged signs of intelligence which made Hippolyte all the more uneasy as he was winning. But, in the end, a last trick made the two lovers the baroness's debtors. As he was looking for change in his pocket, the painter took his hands off the table, and then saw in front of him a purse which Adélaide had slipped there, without his noticing it. The poor girl was holding the old one and to save face was looking in it for money to pay her mother. All Hippolyte's blood rushed so quickly to his heart that he nearly fainted. The new purse which had replaced his own and which contained his fifteen louis was embroidered with gold beads. The knots, the tassels, everything bore witness to Adélaide's good taste. She had no doubt used all her savings to pay for the ornaments on this charming piece of work. It was impossible to say more delicately that the painter's gift could only be rewarded with a token of affection. When Hippolyte, overcome with joy, turned his eyes to Adélaide and the baroness, he saw them trembling with pleasure, happy at this kindly trick. He felt petty, mean and foolish. He would have liked to be able to punish himself, to rend his heart. Tears came into his eyes, and, impelled by an irresistible feeling he got up, took Adélaide in his arms, pressed her against his heart, kissed her and then, with an artist's directness, exclaimed looking at the baroness, 'I ask you for her hand in marriage.'

Adélaide looked at the painter half angrily and Madame de Rouville, somewhat surprised, was thinking what to say in reply when the scene was interrupted by the sound of the doorbell. The old vice-admiral appeared followed by his shadow and Madame Schinner. Having guessed the reason for the sorrows which her son tried in vain to hide from her, Hippolyte's mother had made inquiries about Adélaïde from some of her friends. Rightly alarmed at the slanders which maligned the girl without the Comte de Kergarouet's knowledge, Madame Schinner (who had learned his name from the caretaker) had been to tell the vice-admiral about them. In his rage he said he wanted 'to cut off the brutes' ears'. Excited by his anger, the admiral had told Madame Schinner the secret of his voluntary losses at cards, since the baroness's pride allowed him only this ingenious method of helping her.

When Madame Schinner had greeted Madame de Rouville, the latter looked at the Comte de Kergarouet, the Chevalier du Halga (the former admirer of the late Comtesse de Kergarouet), Hippolyte and Adélaïde, and said with the graciousness of true feeling, 'It seems that we are a family party this evening.'

PENGUIN 60s CLASSICS